THE FEARLESS EYE

AIZEN MALKI

Dedicated to all who have the courage and passion to spread love in a world that doesn't encourage it often enough. For you.

The Fearless Eye

Copyright © 2018

Second Edition

This is a work of fiction. Names, characters, businesses, organizations, places, events, and incidents either are a product of the author's imagination or are used fictionally. Any resemblance to persons, living or dead, is purely coincidental.

ISBN 978-0-692-12693-6

Cover art done by Jacob Meyer – Edit by BimawithPencil

Printed in the United States of America

For more information or inquiries visit www.Aizenmalki.com

Thank you for your cooperation

Many more worlds to come

CHAPTER 0

The Beginning

The metropolitan rooftop was an escape. A welcomed departure from the pragmatic confinements of responsibility. A place to let your mind flow. Not in front of you, but above you. Up into the endless void that was the sky. The darkness holds just enough mystery to keep us watching. And it kept eleven-year-old Samuel watching. Watching and wondering.

His fifteen-year-old brother Roger opened the door from the stairway cut onto the rooftop. He noticed Samuel and approached.

"What are you always looking at up here? Not like you can see stars in the city." Samuel's eyes didn't break away from the pitch-black blanket above.

"I can too."

"Oh yeah? If you can point to a single star, I'll shut up."

Samuel pointed upward without hesitation.

"Uh ... I don't see anything Sam.... You must be watching too many holovids—"

"Just because you can't see them doesn't mean they're not there," Samuel replied quickly. Roger's sass turned into a smile.

"Got me there, little brother. You win." Samuel looked over at Roger, now peering out at the sky.

"Well ... why do you come out here if there's nothing to see?" Samuel asked. Roger's smile dissolved a bit.

"It's the only time we can look up."

A blistering hot sun beat down heavily with unrelenting, oppressive passion. The world lay more barren in recent years, desperately hoping to fend off the force of nature from baking it like Scotch eggs.

The family car rolled by, on its way to a roofed drop-off area. The roof was lined completely with solar panels, and the sides were blocked off, to keep the kids inside or the sun out.

Samuel and Roger jumped down and made their way inside. They broke away from each other with a wave as Samuel found his classroom. His favorite class, Science & Technology.

Samuel sat down at his seat, front of the class, and put his dinosaur-themed lunchbox on the floor next to him. The teacher waited for the chatter to die down and then began his lesson.

"With the new discoveries in astrophysics, it would seem that one day, travel to other worlds filled with life could be a very real possibility. We just have to figure out a way to get there. . . . But maybe we should do something about our planet first, huh?" Samuel's face lit up with a subtle awe.

After a short lesson, the teacher walked over to Samuel's desk as he passed out papers. He took notice of the boy's fascination, brandishing a smirk of his own. The page hit his desk.

The same page, now existing in a folder as more of a keepsake than anything else. A reminder in the folder to a five-year-older Samuel. A Samuel with a burning passion within him. A Samuel with a project to present.

The classroom awaited his words. The teacher gave a certain hand gesture, signifying his time to begin. Samuel cleared his throat with a smile. He presented, barely taking a moment to breathe in between his points.

"In conclusion, this will make a difference in how people are able to live comfortably and not succumb to the heat, especially in developing countries." He looked up, seemingly for the first time, and noticed nobody had been paying attention. The teacher clapped a few times in pity.

"A nice idea. A bit idealistic. How does this . . . uh . . . relate to ending the war though, Samuel?" Samuel looked on, anxiety setting in.

"Well . . . uh. Maybe it could unite people. Help everyone come together against something we all deal with—"

"That wasn't necessarily what this project was about to begin with. And secondly, *probably most importantly*, the science isn't quite there. To create something like that, you'd need a dozen nuclear powerplants. And crossing borders isn't quite the safest thing to do right now. . . ." The silence added weight to Samuel's embarrassment. The teacher realized he had crushed the boy, but didn't care quite enough to retract any of his statements. He settled for a bit of padding.

"Optimistic approach though. Either way. Thank you. Who's next?" Samuel looked around the room, displeased. He rubbed his fingers together in a nervous twitch, then gripped his notepad tightly in frustration. They didn't care about what he had to say. *Nobody did.*

Samuel, still steaming, clutched his backpack tightly as he walked down the hall. A young girl's voice called out to him.

"Hey, Sam!" Samuel stopped walking. A hint of nervousness crept into him. He turned around to see Ariel's

4

ocean blue eyes staring up at him, almost hiding underneath her thick, blonde hair.

"Hey, Ariel. What's u—"

"Well? How'd it go?" Samuel paused to form the right face to aid his lie.

"It went well. Mr. Ementior thought it was a great idea."

"That's awesome, Sam! Knew it would go well." Samuel tried his best to match her genuine happiness toward him. But all he could manage was a hollow smile. Empty; with only the success of his goals being truly able to fill it.

"I'll show them. They'll all have to understand one day," Samuel thought, tightening his grip once again.

A single light loomed over the table as a deal was struck. A man shrouded in the darkness, just outside of the bulb's illuminance, whispered to his interpreter.

"Our stance hasn't wavered. What we choose to use Dr. Kaine's blueprints for is none of your concern. Our offer stands," said the interpreter with unwavering conviction.

Samuel, now thirty, sported an ill-kept beard and greased, wavy, shoulder-length hair. He looked on, pressured to make a choice.

"We're, uh . . . going to need consistent funding. Research, development, distribution." Whispers were heard from the end of the table hidden in darkness once again.

"It will be done."

Sweat trickled down the brow of a now thirty-five-old Samuel. He was tall, fit, and sported neatly trimmed, medium-length, dark-brown hair and beard, with thick, black-framed glasses. It was hotter than you'd imagine in a rural African village.

Workers wearing the same raised, hexagon-adorned jumpsuits as Samuel unloaded advanced-looking solar equipment from boxes labeled "Roger Kaine Innovations." Samuel watched on proudly. He was in charge of the operation. Suddenly, he was called into a meeting room.

Samuel entered, looking the stern man many years his senior square in his murky, yellowed eyes. His skin, clearly damaged from the sun. His body, dehydrated. Samuel sat down at the other end of the table.

The man hunched over the paperwork in front of him, troubled. Guards surrounded him, standing idly by. He was the leader of the village.

"If we accept these terms . . . these resources, . . . we give up—" Samuel cut him off.

"I'd say you've got a lot more to give up if you *don't* accept the terms." Samuel's terse, almost uncaring eyes met the leaders' once again. The man's gazed gripped tightly to Samuel's. He knew he had no choice.

A soft female voice radiated from outside the tent like a siren. It called for Samuel.

"Samuel," the voice whispered. Samuel's eyes widened. He quickly shuffled outside to see a near angelic-looking woman in a summer dress standing with a pre-teen boy and girl at each of her sides. Samuel's breath slowed as he approached in near disbelief. He looked at both kids, which only furthered his confusion.

"Samuel," the voice whispered once again. Fire subtly formed around the edge of Samuel's vision. After a moment, everything in sight suddenly engulfed into a violent blaze, including himself.

GASP. Samuel shot up from his bed. A nightmare. All too real. Not far from the truth he knew.

CHAPTER 1

The Experiment

I ran my trembling fingers through my unkempt hair. I had been sweating in my sleep. I looked down at my hands. No burns. *"These nightmares will be the death of me,"* I thought. A deep-red glow reflected on my face.

My monitor mounted on the wall played footage from a news channel. It was an intense fire burning a skyscraper to ashes. The reporter's words quietly echoed around my empty, minimalistic, concrete apartment.

"It's beyond our control. And sources say there's no putting it out. . . . The Pentagon has confirmed what we've feared. It's reached us. It's at our doorstep—" I sunk into bed, trying to tune it out. An expected tragedy. My eyes darted around anxiously. A light illuminated from my nightstand. A small, holographic envelope with the number fourteen in the corner appeared and then then disappeared. It reappeared. Fifteen now.

I poked at it to bring up the messages.

Roger:

Sam.

Will you answer already?

Come to the lab.... No sense being alone with what's happening....

I paused for a moment and exhaled. I slid out of bed and planted my feet on the cold floor. I reached into my closet to grab one of only a few different choices of the heat-resistant jumpsuits. Black. Always black. Just before walking out of my room, I took one last look at the monitor. The building burned to the ground.

Fires burned all over the planet. One in the distance reflected on the surface of Roger Kaine's glasses as he gazed out of his laboratory window. He stared out at the world as if he himself had caused its pain. He touched a button on his wheelchair, wheeling away slowly. As the only family he (or I) had left, I watched him in agony. The atmosphere was dark, grey, and on the verge of nonexistence. Toxic chemicals had been dispersed around densely populated areas, plaguing the Earth with decay.

Roger ran his fingers across the delicate leaves of the plant he grew under a special heating lamp. He had genetically modified it, spending years on its design, making for a spectacular sight; blood-red leaves with bright branches. He treated the plant as if it were his child.

He turned to face me, staring for a moment before speaking.

"The war is here, even more so than they're letting on. Who knows how long humanity has . . . ? How much longer we have?"

I always respected Roger's words, his foresight and perspective. After all, he was the one who had truly become the scientist. Not me. I was better at . . . dealing with people. But it wasn't until he spoke about how bleak and grim the situation was that it really, *truly* sunk in how little time we had left. My heart sped up.

"There's nothing we can do . . . can we?" I asked, hopelessness leaking from my tone. Roger took a few moments to answer once again.

"I-I've asked a lot of you over the years. But maybe there *is* . . . something to be done. . . . Can I ask you of one more thing?" he asked with powerfully locked eye contact. I sighed. Not out of being fed up with him, no. But out of lack of belief. *What could we do now? Haven't we done enough?*

"Sure, Roger, go ahead." He then rolled over to a towering object hiding under a large blue tarp; the same kind that, before we were able to fully prevent weather disasters, used to cover houses damaged by hurricanes or tornadoes. He grabbed the tarp with one hand.

"I want you to be a part of my very last experiment." Roger yanked the covering off. There stood a rather impressive looking device appearing to be made mostly of diamond or some other crystal. The machine intensified the ceiling lights as they refracted through it, creating a marvelous pattern of light. I admired in awe.

"What is it?" I noticed a separate crystal shard encased within a chamber at the base of the machine. I pointed to it.

"Wait . . . is this?" Roger wheeled closer to Samuel.

"Yes. It is. Unlike anything this world's ever seen. . . . Made this machine using it, in secret. It-It's meant to send one outside the boundaries of space and time."

"What does that even mean, Roger?" Lights on the machine's control panel began to flicker.

"It means that where you end up is guided by your consciousness." I shook my head.

"Einstein of our generation or not, your inventions still scare the hell out of me."

"I want you to use it, Sam. . . . This might be your only chance . . . of survival. I don't know where you'll end up. But there are millions of planets in the universe. And anywhere other than this godforsaken planet will do."

I stared blankly in anxiety, running through the possibilities in my head. Just like any other human, I feared the unknown more than anything. I rubbed my fingers together. Clammy.

"I just . . . have so many questions. How will I know the machine won't just kill me instantly? What if the place isn't habitable? I just don't—"

"I tested on mice initially. Scanned their brains before and while the machine was turned on. Noticed something. It was as if the readings on the machine matched those coming from their brain. As if . . . the machine was being guided by the rat. . . . And then they vanished. . . ." I broke eye contact and pondered more, trying to keep from being overwhelmed. Roger continued.

"I'd go myself, but I fear my own pessimistic mind might . . . but you, Samuel. You've always been a dreamer. A believer. Haven't you." I shuffled a bit uncomfortably, still in doubt.

"Look, Sam . . . I can't promise you anything. But I can tell you that if it works like it should, this *is* your last chance at escaping. And my last-ditch effort to save your life. . . . Go through with this. . . . **Live.**" I was petrified with thought and remained silent.

An explosion echoed through the air, far in the distance. I nervously shot my gaze out the window but was interrupted.

"It's this or DIE, Sam!" he added ferociously. My attention was magnetized to Roger once again. This was it, wasn't it? I needed to make a decision. My thoughts were on fire with blazing consideration.

I ran my hand through my coarse facial hair and then slowly exhaled to calm my vigorous heartbeat. I looked at Roger's chair, his nonexistent legs and hunched posture. He hated whenever somebody took pity on him. But pity would often escape the filters of my mind. He never married. And never had children either. But I guess, for that matter, neither did I. But for different reasons. The accident had left him impotent. A reality even the most gifted scientific mind couldn't erase. I blinked deeply and put a hand on Roger's shoulder.

"Alright . . . I'll do it," Roger revealed a quick, pleased smile before turning around to work the machine without a moment to waste. After a second or two of screen pushing and digital knob turning, Roger nodded.

"Wait. I'm leaving now?" I asked with much disquiet.

"Yes, you must leave now. Who knows if we'll even survive the night!" I couldn't sneak a word in before he continued.

"The machine is activating, and you might only have one chance for this to work! On the platform. Walk under the sensor." I squinted at Roger.

"You know me. You activated it now because you knew if I had time, I'd overthink it." Roger smiled and nodded as he continued to prepare the machine.

A walkway made of crystal illuminated. At the end of the walkway, a platform waited with a light shining down, emitting from a large crystal chunk.

*"Am I ready for this? Could I **ever** be ready for this?"*

I attempted a hug. We hadn't done enough of those. Roger nodded a lonely nod and put his arms out while looking down. We embraced for all but a moment. Not enough time. Never enough time.

The machine whirled with intimidating hisses. It seemed fully powered up.

"It's ready, Sam. . . . Best to clear your mind. Completely." I nodded. He continued.

"Maybe it's best you don't bring any emotion in there, actually. Don't want your fears to hitch a ride. . . ."

I searched my psyche for last-minute inner peace. I tried the hardest I could to find reasons why I shouldn't be afraid of where I would end up. I trusted my brother. I knew anything he created would work efficiently. All the more terrifying.

I took in some more deep breaths. I had mediated a time or two. I had to put those skills to the test.

Once I stepped onto the translucent platform in front of the crystal generator, it lit up a deep, smoky purple underneath me. I paced toward the circular, pitch-black hole that would take me into the unknown. The outer rim shined like the blinding sliver of sun in a solar eclipse. I squinted harshly into the light as bright as my hope for survival. I slowly put my first foot ahead, and then the rest of my body followed.

Staring into the black, empty void was intimidating, but at this point, I was fearless. I had to be. I gritted my teeth and nodded silently.

I turned back to look at Roger one final time. He smiled a broken smile and raised his hand to wave.

"Any last words for this dying world?" he asked. I looked at all he had become. He was always going to be the brother I knew as a child. The big brother on that rooftop. The one who entertained my dreams for the world, even if they were pipedreams in the end. Even if they . . . did more harm than good. I felt strange; a feeling I didn't quite understand. As if I wasn't actually leaving him after all. He would be with me no matter what.

"Goodbye, Roger. Despite all that's happened, you were always a great brother to me." A small tear slid down Roger's cheek. It reflected the light emitted from the machine. I smiled and turned to leave on that note when I hesitated for a moment. I sighed. After exhaling smoothly, I said, "If you ever do see Ariel again, tell her that I'll always love her. And that if there really are any kids out there, that I love them too." Roger's eyes widened. He nodded.

I cleared my mind entirely once again and reached out into the dark abyss ahead. The very moment my middle finger touched the inside of the portal, the crystal casing started to glow and flash rapidly. A wave of heat drifted out from within the machine, and before I could utter another word, I was immediately sucked inside of it.

I was instantaneously overcome by a force felt all over my body and beyond. Unlike anything I had ever experienced. My consciousness felt as though it died and was reborn thousands of times within a fraction of a perceivable moment. I couldn't even recollect who I was or if I should even attempt to do so. My thoughts peeled away at each other like splintering chips of wood and sawdust.

Pure mental force enveloped me. I couldn't feel my body nor did I ever ponder about what a body really was until that moment. I was energy without a vessel, simply floating in an empty space of senseless desire amidst wonder and endless imagination. Among everything I thought I'd feel, I would never have guessed that whirling through the depths of space and time could make me feel so free.

THE FEARLESS EYE

Journal Entry #5

Mom wants me to do these dumb vocal journals once a week, and I never know what to say on them. She tells me to talk about what I feel. Well, I'll tell you how I feel. The kids at school are all stupid. I think. They just. I dunno. They're dumb. Every time I say something, it's like they find a way to make me feel weird for even thinking it. It's not like I can't do all the stuff they do. I kick the ball farther than most of them. I even hit the park dome cover once! And that's pretty high! But I just . . . Sometimes . . . I feel like I should just not say anything. Not talk at all or something. I don't know. Maybe if I don't say anything, they won't be able to pick everything apart. Maybe I'll try that for a while. There is somebody I might be ok to talk to though. . . . She's really nice. Nicer than all the others.

THE FEARLESS EYE

CHAPTER 2

The New World

All understanding of time was completely lost on me. I could have been floating within the dark void for hours, days, years, centuries before coming to a complete stop. Suddenly, I felt a soft thump as my feet slowly touched ground. I was momentarily blinded, didn't hear a sound, and I was unable to taste or smell as well as I normally could. Touch, being the first of the five senses I regained, allowed me to notice the bitter chill spearing through my body like a frozen blade. Goosebumps rose by the hundreds across my body. I wore one layer of thin clothing, which was made to cope with the extreme temperature of Earth's planetary state, yet I found myself in weather at least 80 degrees Fahrenheit cooler.

All of a sudden, my stomach turned violently within me. I kneeled over and stumbled to the ground. The whole area around my stomach pulsated at an alarming rate. I immediately vomited with unrelenting force. I kept at it until I was reduced to spitting up my stomach's digestive fluid. My eyes watered and my nose began to run. I could feel my sense of taste coming back as the bitter flavor of liquid leaving my esophagus hit my palette. I laid down on the cold, rough terrain and tried to take deep breaths.

After a few moments, I attempted to get up normally; but being weakened by the endless discharge, it was a struggle to rise to my feet again. Not knowing where I was, I desperately wanted to regain my vision. My eyes weren't shut, but my sight appeared as though I had looked directly at the sun for too long. A plethora of color flashed before my weakened eyes as I blinked heavily and rubbed away the discomfort.

Before long, I began to see more than just a blur of color. I looked around at my new surroundings.

Lush hillsides and mossy trees lined the terrain. The grassy fields felt untouched and uncultivated; wild and full of life. Plant life, that is. The clouds were thin, long, and flat. Their jobs were to cover the tiny sun hiding away as if it wanted nothing to do with the planet. A bizarre juxtaposition to how green everything was. There were rocky mountains in the distance with a good amount of snow covering the peaks.

My sense of sound went back to normal as faint breezes of wind passed by my ice-cold ears. After my full strength and the rest of my senses returned, I decided to wander out in search of any form of life. I walked aimlessly. My head moved from left to right as I scanned the area around me for anything worth heading toward. The quiet valley delivered a message of loneliness and fear for survival. Yet it was beautiful. Peaceful even. It almost made me miss the old days of Earth from my childhood.

I remembered running through the greenhouse my parents would routinely take me and my brother to. The soft touch of the warm sun on my bare shoulders made me feel like I was growing along with the moist plants inside the massive structure. With various plant species and a diverse collection of flowers scattered around, I always had something to look at, something to analyze.

Where I grew up, the sun shined brightly, and we would sweat profusely while barely moving. As blazing hot as that was, the temperature only intensified as the years rolled on.

The memory was disturbed by an involuntary shiver. I realized the danger I was truly in. Hypothermia was knocking.

I walked for miles before I found a small cave at the base of a mountain. There was a narrow stream running toward the other side of the range. I was parched and drank until my throat was content. The water was crystal clear, allowing me to notice something peculiar. As I put my hands into the water, my eyes darted back and forth. I squinted to get a more precise look. There wasn't a single fish or any sign of life in the water. I was puzzled. I couldn't understand why there wouldn't be animal life in a river between mountains. A worrying sign.

"*What if there isn't any animal life on this planet? How will I eat?*" My thoughts raced as I started to feel hungrier by the minute. I hadn't even seen a bird in the air the entire time I had been here. It was then I decided to camp out for a while, warm up, and later cut through the canyon in the hope of finding some sort of food source.

I gathered up the few stray branches I could find and assembled them correctly. Luckily, I had gone on plenty of camping trips with my family growing up. I used to love the outdoors. I found myself feeling happier and more peaceful while out there. The smell of the Earth and the sound of the crackling fire served as a way to bring troubles of daily life to a halt. It was a much needed respite from reality; a welcomed unity with my surroundings.

As the fire grew larger, I nearly smothered it with my body in a desperate attempt to heat myself up. The flame flickered, bouncing light off of the rugged walls of the small cave. I rubbed my hands together hastily. My tired eyes stared into the center of the glowing pile of warmth in front of me. Perhaps it held the answers because I knew my mind didn't.

"Why did I end up *here?*" I said aloud. I scratched my beard nervously.

After a short rest, I got up with a deep exhale. I needed nutrients, or I wouldn't last long.

I got a couple more sips of water in before an idea struck me. If I followed the stream through the mountains, perhaps I would find civilization. Where there is water, there is life. I decided to literally bet my life on that principle. I nodded and began my ascent, walking alongside the stream, occasionally looking down in the hope I would see a wild salmon carelessly swimming about. I wondered why I hadn't properly prepared for a situation like this.

"I should have brought some sort of backpack with materials and food. Why wasn't this thought of?" Perhaps my mind was preoccupied with fear and curiosity. On top of that, everything happened so fast, which made packing lunch the last thing I was worried about.

I hadn't expected this planet to be like Earth, but it sure did seem similar to it in many ways. The only thing "alien" about it that I could tell was one particular tree. Somewhat shorter than the rest and rather lanky with florescent-green bark and crimson leaves shaped in perfect circles. One of the most peculiar things I had ever seen. Even more so, there were what looked like small fruits in a star-like shape forming off of it. I wasn't quite ready to resort to eating purple alien fruit. But at least it was an option.

I pressed on; and after miles of walking, I finally reached the end of the mountain range. I peered out about 100 meters ahead and staggered. I marveled at what was before my eyes.

I was looking at what appeared to be a village comprised of eighteen individual pyramids. Each pyramid was comparable to the size of a capacious, three-story house. They all looked exactly the same, identical in size, color, and the amount of space between each one I wasn't sure what they were made of, but I could tell they were all built with the same material. They were all bright white in color and didn't seem to have any imperfections in their design.

The walls didn't look like they were made of individual blocks either. They looked smooth, as if each wall was its own respective piece. They were all perfectly stacked and constructed to be the exact same as their neighbors'. The layout of the village was a row of three individual pyramids, then six, then nine. At the angle I looked, I couldn't tell if they had doors or windows, but the tip of each pyramid seemed to be translucent, indicating they were made by some sort of advanced intelligent life.

Despite that, all of the walls were covered in mossy vines. Could be due to abandonment. Could be due to the desire to integrate nature into the lives of the citizens. I was getting ready to walk toward the dwellings when some very important questions arose in my now perplexed brain.

"How do I even approach these people? What will they think of me, and how will they react to my presence? What if these beings are vicious killers? How will they understand what I say?" I was glad I stopped before I did anything rash, but now I faced a serious dilemma.

"Why don't people ever ask themselves things like this in movies?" I thought with a nervous chuckle.

I only saw two options. Just waltz through the center of town like I belong there, or sneak around their homes and try to confront one alone. My stomach and its growing hunger encouraged me to move at a fast pace, but my brain saw patience and caution to be the right way to go about it.

"I can't eat if I'm already imprisoned or dead," I said aloud.

I laid down so that only my eyes and the very top of my head were exposed from their point of view. I waited patiently for movement of any kind.

As minutes turned into an hour, a heavy blanket of darkness covered my new planet. With a bulbous blanket of clouds covering the sky, it was difficult to see my hands in front of me. The only source of visible light were crystals growing out of the ground. Marvelous shades of electric blue lined them in a natural yet unearthly level of beauty. I didn't allow my logic of approach to be soiled by my admiration for the spectacle.

"Just because their village is a sight to see doesn't mean their friendly, Sam," I thought.

At this point, I was much colder than I had been during the day, and fatigue started to get to me. I figured lighting another fire and then sleeping the night away would be the best choice for me. I walked a bit further away from the town to make sure the glow of light would be impossible for them to see. After gathering my materials and lighting my new fire, I laid down on the cold, rough ground under another one of the outlandish trees with the unusual colors. I took a deep breath and then closed my eyes.

I searched myself for mental comfort. All I could think of was Ariel. I daydreamed about how she would squint her eyes nearly shut every time she laughed. Her smile, radiant and contagious. Her long, straight, blonde hair glistened in the sunlight as if it was literally glowing. She was wittier than most, always figuring me out. Couldn't hide anything from her for long. Time went by faster than it ever had before. By the time we were in our mid-twenties and out of college, we were in love and ready to marry. Until . . .

I shifted in discomfort. I opened my eyes and gazed out at the sky. The clouds had separated just enough for me to peek at the stars. They were so vibrant and well defined they almost looked fake. I had never seen a night sky like it before. It was as if I peered into the eyes of the cosmos itself. I sighed a thoughtful sigh. Whatever the next day held for me, I just hoped it didn't contain hunger, imprisonment, or death.

CHAPTER 3

The Encounter

I woke up to what appeared to be around 8 or 9 a.m. I struggled to find my glasses I had placed next to me just before falling asleep. I reached for them with naturally shaky hands and stretched my tense limbs as I sat up. Pain in my lower back shot through my body, causing me to stumble while getting to my feet.

I looked up at the sky. It was the same as the day before. Dull and uneventful with the sun trapped under the clouds' careful guard. For some reason, I desperately wanted to see the sun. Though I was physically alone, it was the absence of the large star's warmth making me feel lonely. I had spent most of my life trying to protect the planet from it, and here I was craving it. Enough irony to carve a smirk on my face.

I shivered. I hadn't felt cold at all as I had slept. I was so exhausted from traveling planet to planet that it would have taken an attack from a bear to wake me.

I stretched one more time, and then something caught the very edge of my peripheral vision. The tree with the odd colors looked different. The deep-red leaves dimly glowed, and the bright-green branches appeared fuzzy. I cleaned my glasses and then moved in for a closer look. The hazy blur on the branches had been caused by remarkably thin hairs now all stretching as far outward as possible. As I gazed at the incredible sight, I noticed something interesting. As time passed, the leaves glowed brighter and brighter.

After a minute or two, they glowed bright enough to be seen from a couple of hundred meters away. That thought reminded me of something. The tree was tall enough to be seen over the cliff, with a gradual grade out by where the pyramids were.

"What if this glowing tree attracts their attention?"

I immediately snapped out of amazement and scurried off into some nearby bushes. I decided to wait there for ten minutes. If nothing showed up, I would leave and try to find a way around the village, hopefully running into a native creature by itself.

I waited for the self-promised ten minutes, and just as I was getting ready to get up and run, *I saw it*. It casually walked up the ridge toward the tree. I kneeled down lower.

It softly reached for one of the fruits. It plucked it with grace. The moment the fruit detached, a low hum vibrated through the very vessel of my existence. I felt as though the sound was heard through my soul and inside of my body rather than by my ears. I focused my sight on what was in front of me. For the very first time, I laid my eyes on an intelligent life form other than a human being.

I was completely and utterly fascinated by its presence. It appeared to be similar to a naked human man without genitals. It was about six feet tall, had long arms and small hands that seemed disproportionate. It was totally hairless, and its body was slim and lean. I also noticed it didn't have an Adam's apple. Its skin color was pale-white and looked flawlessly clean and untouched. It didn't have any type of birthmarks, scars, or noticeable veins protruding from its skin, despite being so thin.

Up until now, I had only seen the side of its body as it consumed the fruit. It had put it into where I thought its mouth would be. I tried to be as silent as possible, but I knelt down in an unusual position that my feet weren't used to. I suddenly felt my muscles tighten and quickly contract. I got a severe cramp on the arch of my right foot causing me to stumble a bit. My movement created a rustling sound in the group of bushes I hid in. The being gently turned its head in my direction. My heart beat faster than it ever had before. I sweated cold bullets, and my palms were as wet as morning dew.

It lowered its arms from the tree and nonchalantly walked closer to where I was. At this point, I saw its entire face for the first time. The only thing about it that wasn't completely white, grey, or black was a small, triangular-shaped area just above the eyes in the center of its forehead glowing bright purple. Its eyes were striking. Its sclerae were entirely black and had a glossy shine to them. Its irises were pure white, and its pupils were almost too small to notice. Even though it couldn't see me, I felt as though it looked deeply into my very being. Its jawline and chin were chiseled and fine. Its nose was pointy, small, and thin just like its ears. Its lips were the same color as its skin, and the width of them was also slimmer than a human's. In addition to being bald, it didn't have any eyebrows or eyelashes. It had a blank, emotionless expression that struck an unfamiliar fear within me.

I had to think quickly. *"What are my options?"* My mind raced as fast as my blood pressure rose. Adrenaline pumped through my system at an alarming rate. I started to panic. The fear of this creature pushed me off the edge of prudence, as I was no longer concealing my presence.

"What if it comes over and attacks me?! Maybe I should attack it," I thought to myself wildly. My eyes darted back and forth in contemplation.

I decided to show myself. I jetted my head upward first, and then the rest of my body. Its expression was unchanged. I wondered how and why it wasn't surprised to see me. Or at the very least, startled by my movements.

It continued on its path toward me, now extending his hand out in my direction. The hand formed into a finger. The closer it got, the more frightened I became. Its energy almost had its own gravitational pull. It was powerful. Could be . . . dangerous.

"What will happen if this creature touches me?! I'm not going to find out the hard way!"

Then, in a frenzy of delirium, I leaped out of the bushes and tackled the being. We made a loud thump as we hit the ground. It didn't resist at all; how easily it went down scared me. It showed no sign of refusal. As soon as it was pinned, I rushed to get up and backed off a few feet. It sat up a bit and glanced over at me. Its facial expression had not changed one bit. It was like the attack hadn't fazed it whatsoever. I backed up a few more feet. My brain tried its hardest to clamp onto an answer.

"What's wrong with it?" I questioned. *"Why didn't it react to me at all?"* I couldn't come to any conclusions. Sweat slowly trickled over my temple. The being looked directly into my fearful eyes. It was completely still and looked as if it had no intention of harming me.

"What are you?!" I yelled. I felt like a petrified animal. A barely evolved ape man in the woods. Again, it didn't flinch and merely looked at me with the same expression.

"How will it even understand me? Perhaps my tone of voice is crucial," I thought. I waited a few seconds and then calmed down a hair.

"I am a . . . human . . . from the planet Earth. I've come here to live. I don't mean to harm any of you. I just want to survive."

The moment I was done speaking, the being stood back up. I gritted my teeth and, although terrified, stood my ground. Despite my first attack, it approached me again, arm outstretched. As it got closer, I walked backward, eventually tripping over a small rock that caused me to fall to the ground. The six-foot creature stood over me with an impeccable presence. Its watchful eyes burned a hole into my shield of defense, leaving only distress behind. Seeing the being loom above my shaking human body scared me more than anything ever had before. I was too frightened to move. I squeezed my eyes shut like a horror-stricken child and hoped for it to all be over quickly.

I waited for some sort of strike, but it never came. I opened my eyes and looked up at my large foe. Instead, it had its hand inches away from my face, just above my eye level. It gently touched the center of my forehead where the triangle marking would have been on me if I had one. Suddenly, its purple triangle started to glow softly again. I didn't feel anything in particular, but I was under the impression it was doing something to me.

I mustered up the courage to shove it away. This time, it crashed to the ground harder, and it even had a shred of preservation for its safety, landing with its arms out. It was breathing much harder than before and appeared to have its eyes wide open. It retracted its arm and put both of its hands on its head. It slowly started to grip its head tighter and tighter. Its purple triangle of light, as well as the leaves on the colored tree, began to wildly flicker their colors from bright to dim.

After about a minute or two of heavy breathing and head grasping, it did something in every way unexpected. The creature hunched over toward the left, opened its mouth, and screamed with all its might. It cried out for as long as it could. Around the very end, I could hear its voice getting clearer, much deeper, and more human-like. The light emitting from its forehead covered the whole area in a fog-like aura of purple glow. I couldn't take my eyes off of it. Whatever it was doing, it was something I couldn't have ever imagined I would encounter before walking through that portal.

When the screaming subsided, the being stood up straight and lowered its hands down to its shoulders. It looked back at me, and then at its hands. I quivered as I watched it obliquely grin with its thin lips. It emoted for the first time, striking me with immense discomfort. The smile was shrewd and disturbing. It looked as though it had made a nefarious discovery and was overcome by it. The being glanced over at me one last time. It studied me with this new, wicked expression on its face. I didn't know what to expect. I suggested running, but before I got the chance to get up, he turned around and started walking toward the town of pyramids.

"What is it going to do now?" Despite what I had just gone through, I just . . . **had** to follow him. I felt absolutely compelled to. I would be sneaky about it though. I couldn't let him detect my presence.

I waited a few minutes before setting out after him. I figured following too closely wasn't the right move. He was walking toward the center of town. Being around a quarter mile away, it was time to get closer before I lost him.

I kept close to the edge of the town, hiding behind one of the pyramids. I pressed my back up against the ice-cold wall. My heart began to progressively beat faster again. I ran my fingers through my hair, wiping my sweaty forehead on the way up. I had forgotten about hunger or how cold I was. Being absorbed in curiosity, all I could focus on was this unbelievable situation I was in, and how it was just a day before this that I slept in my bed on Earth. I inhaled hard with my nose, waited until my lungs were completely full, paused for a second or two, and then exhaled slowly. I paced my breathing for a few more seconds and consciously tried to slow my heart rate. I could feel myself calming down. I put my hand on my chest and felt the thumps become less frequent. It was time for me to act again.

CHAPTER 4

The Epidemic

I slid over to the side of the pyramid. My curiosity drove me, dragged me to the situation I found myself in. I had just seen something no man had ever dreamed of seeing. I couldn't look away now. Peeled.

I poked my head out and glanced over toward the being. I noticed all of the pyramids had at least two eight-foot doorways: one facing toward the pyramid in front, the other toward the one directly next to it. The town started to look like one big structure at this point. As if it was a collective shelter for all beings to share. I directed my attention back to the being. It walked toward the center of the town, but suddenly stopped. Within a few moments, I saw a faint glow emitting from just above its head. It was a purple light similar to the triangular marking on the being's forehead I had seen before.

After thirty seconds or so, the glow began to fade, followed by other identical beings coming out of their individual pyramids in unison. There were seventeen of them including the original being. As they drew closer to it, I saw it look around as if it analyzed each of the individuals differently. It had its eyes set on one in particular. It happened to be the one that came out of the pyramid in front of the only vacant one, which I guessed belonged to the original being.

It moved closer to the newer one and in a flash did the unthinkable. The original grabbed the new being by the neck, squeezed for a moment, and threw it to the ground with unrelenting force. My grip on the pyramid wall tightened. From completely relinquishing the idea of resistance against my primitive attack to committing such a violent act in this short a period of time was everything but what I expected.

The other being laid there for about as long as the original had after I tackled it. After getting up, the first then put its hand on the triangular mark in the center of the second's forehead. The purple light shined much brighter this time. The two of them seemed to be within each other's glow.

After half of a minute, the light slowly dimmed back to normal opacity. The new being looked directly into the original's eyes, then turned to the being to its left. Without a shred of hesitation, it struck the other being. It fell to the ground without resistance just as the original had. After getting up, it underwent the same process with glowing purple light; yet this time it was the second being performing it on the third. Upon completing the process, the third turned to it in the same exact manner that the second had done. After looking into its eyes, the second turned away from the third and stared directly into the first's eyes again. The third followed the action in perfect unison. The first then raised its two arms in a way to point out to the other beings that had gathered to the center of town as well.

The second and third abruptly shifted their bodies toward the others and began repeating the violent process, attacking three beings total this time. The three newly damaged beings looked toward the second and third and then toward the original once again. The cycle repeated with the three new ones attacking four others. It was then and there I realized what was occurring.

I hid behind the wall again, pushed my back against it, and slid down to the rough terrain. The seemingly unnoticeable pain I felt after falling was nothing compared to the emotional turmoil I felt within me. I put my shaking fingers through my now dirty and coarse hair. I had created this. These beings were naturally fearless. I had gone through the portal with the absence of fear. As a result, I was brought to a place without it.

The first being, when in the presence of my own personal fear, was influenced by it. Changed by it. The purple light must have had something to do with it. After interacting with the others, perhaps they felt fear of it. They looked to the first for direction. The third feared the second, the second feared the first, and in turn the third also feared everything the second did. The original being was the first, followed by two others, and then followed by three others. It was a pyramid. Considering the only structure created by them thus far was a pyramid, I would say it was a concept they find vital. But what was happening before my eyes was disturbing. A spreading of fear itself like a *virus*; a sickness. I had started a pandemic that with time could easily spread.

"What was its plan? Why infect others with fear? What's to gain from it?" I thought. I figured I might find the answers to these questions sooner than later if I didn't get away from the village.

"Are there other villages on this planet? If they were this susceptible to fear, can they be this easily influenced by other emotions?" I pondered. Regardless of possibility, I had to venture out once again. I couldn't be seen. I wasn't sure what this new group of fearful beings would do if they caught me. I had to get out of there.

I stood back up as quietly as possible and took one more peek around the edge of the pyramid. The very second my eyes tried focusing, and before I could even realize what I looked at, one of the beings was directly in my line of sight, within inches of me.

I jerked backward and nearly fell down. It must have been the owner of the pyramid I had been hiding behind the whole time. The being didn't react to my movement at all. It stood there with that same blank expression, allowing me a moment to notice it actually looked somewhat more feminine than the first being. Thinner, with a slightly less chiseled jawline, and narrower shoulders.

Was I ready to accept them and refer to them as something other than "it?"

She had to be among one of the beings who wasn't infected yet. I looked at her again, this time noticing something going on in the town's center behind her. It appeared as though the first being noticed she was missing and directed another being to retrieve her; luckily, he hadn't seen us, and apparently didn't know exactly where we were. I gave her a firm look.

"You're coming with me."

With great impulse and possible momentary regret, I grabbed her by the wrist and began to run back toward the hill I had originally come from. Despite the fact I was dragging her, she ran with me as if she knew I wanted her to. It was convenient to have her go along easily, yet their lack of resistance hadn't failed to creep me out.

As we ran, I wondered how I would describe this all to my brother back home; if I ever ended up back home somehow. I shook my head in disbelief of my situation.

We reached the top of the ridge by the multi-colored tree. I looked behind us to see if we were being followed; nothing. I stopped to think for a moment.

"Should I retrace my steps?" I looked down, only to notice I no longer held the being's wrist. Instead, she approached the tree now flashing in the same fashion as it had when I first encountered the original being. Its branches were even fuzzier than the last time. I squinted in confusion. I took a few steps forward, but then stopped. She reached out and snapped one of the fruits off. I felt the sound vibrate within me again. An indigo-colored sap oozed slowly out of the stem holding the fruit she plucked. It had a wondrous shine to it, fusing the beauty of a kaleidoscope's fractals and the sun itself.

The being put the fruit into her mouth, chewed with a nearly clenched jaw for a lengthy period of time, and then swallowed. Instantly after finishing, the light on her forehead began glowing brighter than I had seen before. She closed her eyes and put her hands out by her hips with her palms facing up. It looked like the colors of the tree were being drawn into her forehead's triangle. The lights dimmed, and she returned to her normal emotionless stance. She turned her head to look at me.

I froze in apparent perplexity. She walked toward me with her hand outstretched. I figured it would be a repeat of what happened before with the original. I accepted this behavior as a natural occurrence at this point, fully allowing her to approach me despite a bit of fear remaining within me.

As she drew closer, I looked deeply into her dark and mysterious eyes. Her blank and emotionless stare hid intense possibility. My heart sped up again, yet the feeling of uneasiness began to leave me the longer I gazed. We came within inches of each other. I swam into the majestic wonders that were her irises. I thought of Ariel. Her beauty reminded me of this new being in an odd sense. I just felt it. It put me at ease. I exhaled calmly and accepted what was coming. She reached out and gently touched my forehead.

The center of my forehead tingled a bit. My brain felt fuzzy and warm from within. I softly shut my eyes. Now that I wasn't distracted by how petrified I was, I focused on the sensation and feeling itself. Spectacular. Filled with positivity and enlightened relief.

Her hand slowly left my forehead after an entire minute. Her eyes widened a bit and her mouth opened slightly. She almost appeared to be in awe of whatever she thought. She looked straight through me for a few moments, but then into my eyes.

I felt a bit nervous considering what happened with the first being. She smiled. It was a great smile; a real smile. It wasn't sinister or devious. I felt relieved. I couldn't help cracking a smile back at her. A lustrous purple mist surrounded us like it had during my first encounter. She took a step backward and peered down at the ground below. She closed her eyes for a second or two, then opened them in unison as her head moved up to look back at me. The smile widened into a grin, exposing her small teeth and creating the first wrinkles her face might have ever experienced. She reached out with both arms and wrapped them around me, embracing me with a warm hug and held still. I felt as if her energy flowed through me. It was like feeling the very fact she was alive. Her life energy itself melded with mine. The whole experience was in every way intense. My heartbeat began to pump away again. Might have been too intense for me, just a human.

She, possibly sensing me feeling overwhelmed, released her hold and took a step back again. Still within a few inches of my face, we stared at each other until she raised her hand to her own face. She put her fingers to her lips, waited a moment, and then raised her arm in the direction of the colorful tree. She then put her hand on my stomach.

"She wants me to eat one of those fruit, doesn't she?" I pondered. I had forgotten about being hungry until I realized what she said. I was starving. It felt like my stomach ate away at its

reserves. To escape the unpleasant feeling and because I really did just want to do what she had told me, I walked over to the tree. My steps were slow and cautious.

"What would this fruit taste like? Is it even compatible with my human digestive system?"

I reached out and, with little to no force, plucked a fruit off of the ever-so-radiant tree. The crimsons and fluorescent greens were far more vibrant up close. The saturation of color, light, and gradients moved me. I looked down at what I held. Merely the size of a golf ball; so small, yet so grand. Truly studying it for the first time revealed it was in the shape of a Merkaba. A three-dimensional, six-pointed star. Like two pyramids intertwined—

"Ah. I see," I thought. I replayed few possible poisonous repercussion scenarios.

"Eating this tiny, seemingly harmless fruit could very well kill me," I mentally proclaimed. But for some reason, even though it defied my cautious and somewhat logical nature, I realized the majority of the events that had taken place since my arrival on the strange planet defied most of what I had ever seen or learned. So what the hell?

I put the fruit to my lips and with the right side of my mouth ground it between my molar teeth. It tasted extremely sour, forcing a violent cough and a grimace. After getting over the nastiness of its taste, something changed that I couldn't put my finger on. I felt it coming on subtly. Within a minute of chewing and swallowing the fruit, my mind began to race to speeds I hadn't experienced before. My brain achieved a new awakening of thought. The very essence of the plant's existence was somehow evident within the shallow frame of my consciousness. Suddenly I could understand the ability I had to feel living things around me, an ability I seemingly possessed *all along.* The revelation of thought served as a beautiful epiphany.

Speechless, I turned to the female being and smiled once again. As I stepped toward her, I noticed my hunger, fatigue, headache, and all other physical issues I'd had vanished. I also wasn't as cold, and even felt a little bit stronger. Magnificent.

I went to reach for another. She softly put her hand on mine, gatekeeping me. I shot a confused glance her way. She shook her head in response. I trusted her judgment.

"Overindulgence isn't advised. Got it." I opened my mouth to speak, but then remembered she wouldn't understand me.

"Hmm. How can I communicate with her?" I questioned aloud. "Perhaps if I talk to her like I normally would a human, she'll pick up on how I feel and react in ways I can comprehend." Before I could, she grabbed my hand as a way to lead me.

"Where are . . . we going?" I stuttered a bit. I squinted at her in hopes she would figure out I was trying to communicate. She closed her eyes and her triangular mark began to glow.

After a few seconds, she turned around, my hand still held in hers, and began walking.

"Following her can't be a bad thing," I thought. *"So long as we're heading in the opposite direction of the village we came from, I'm fine."* It was decided. I would follow her along the path I came on in search of . . . something. Anything, I guess. *"But what am I going to do about what I started?"*

Journal Entry #221

Alright, alright, alright, no choice but to talk about it on here. I got in a fight the other day. Everybody says I started it, but he was talking crap about my brother. Talking about him being in a wheelchair. So screw him! That asshole got what was coming to him! And of course, it just HAD to be one of the guys holding back laughter when I presented in Mr. Ementior's class. And ugh . . . speaking of that. . . . The presentation went . . . horribly. Like, really bad. Mr. E isn't the most positive guy in the room either. Probably not in any room he's ever in. The guy just dumped all over it. I wish I just had a good sarcastic comeback or something. But I always think of that stuff too late. Typical Sam. Ugh. And . . . I . . . shouldn't have lied to Ariel.

CHAPTER 5
The Plan

S he walked at an incredibly slow pace, but I didn't mind much. I was in never-ending awe of her presence. I kept tripping on rocks and small dips in the terrain because I couldn't take my eyes off of her.

We walked for a few hours in complete silence. I thought about the same few things over and over. I reflected on how I ended up on the planet in the first place. The machine was supposed to hurl me through time and space into a setting containing similar aspects to what I felt at the moment of stepping through. Meaning all of the beings I've encountered were fearless from the start; emotionless even. The first being felt fear from our interaction and decided to spread it to the others like a virus. Then I met another blank slate. She was a female I had interacted with ... differently. And so her response was different. She was taking me somewhere. But that's immediately better than, uh . . . choke-slamming me.

I couldn't put my finger on what intention the first being had for doing what did.

"What has he to gain from it all? Power? What will he even do with it?" I pondered.

I scratched the back of my head and sighed. *"I guess I'll just have to see how things play out. I have a feeling that this problem won't be solved so easily,"* I thought.

The being felt no fatigue. She kept the same exact speed the entire time we had been walking, yet my pace progressively slowed. I looked around the mountainous valley for another cave. It was getting late in the day, and the sky had grown dark and cloudless. The beautiful stars showed their faces once again and decided to light our path.

Soon enough, I saw a few large rocks that looked smooth enough to sit on. I sat down, hunched over, and lowered my head. A bit of beaded sweat slipped off of my moist forehead and dispersed into several small drops the moment it hit the ground. I looked down at it. *"Which one can consider itself the original sweat? Or are they all the sweat at the same time?"* I thought. I wondered if I was losing it. I needed to sit and relax my thoughts. Philosophically analyzing my sweat dripping was the last straw.

After a short rest of breathing and hair slicking, I stood back up. I looked over at the being. She had stood in the same spot the entire time I rested; and now that I was up, she continued walking along the path.

We walked on an incline for about thirty minutes until the plateau appeared close. It seemed we reached a cliff similar to the one facing the first village. Suddenly, she stopped and stretched her arm outward in an attempt to point. I caught up and made my way to her side. I looked at her eyes first, but was drawn to her lips. She smiled again.

I turned my head and then peered outward in the direction she pointed in. My mouth opened in awe. A glorious sight was before me. It was a city, *many* times larger than the original. This one went on for over a mile in every direction. It was a metropolis in comparison to the little village I had first encountered. All of the pyramids looked the same except for one. Even though it was in the distance, I could see it was at the very end of the city and was much, much bigger than the rest. There were giant crystals growing directly out of the ground reflecting the stars in the most radiant of ways. There was an abundance of the colorful trees scattered around, and they were all glowing. Based on the past two experiences with the trees, I came to conclude they only brightened when one of the beings approached them; meaning there had to be a plentiful number of other beings within the city.

"If I could just round them all up and have the female being touch them one by one, I could take the whole city by storm." I shook my head to break from the thought.

"Why did I think that?" I asked under my breath. I knew that effectively spreading . . . whatever I did with the female being was better than what that first being was doing. But still wasn't sure what to do.

"Should I be meddling with things? Back on Earth I . . ." I didn't allow myself to finish that thought. I shifted gears into something equally unsettling.

"What happens if a fear-infected being interacts with one of mine? Or me? And what happens if they travel more quickly and spread faster around the planet?" My insides churned. I rubbed my stomach in a hollowed sense of self soothing. I let out a long sigh and lowered my eyelids.

I shifted my eyes over to the left to spy on the actions and expressions of the being. She had brought her arm back to her side, but the smile hadn't left her.

I looked back at the glimmering crystals scattered around the city. They shined so brightly that multiple shadows were cast by each pyramid. Just as I put my first foot forward to head toward the city, I heard a soft thump. I turned back around and found her sitting on the ground. Her posture was perfectly straight with her arms resting on her knees and the bottoms of her feet touching. I watched her in confusion.

"Why would she stop now? We've reached our destination." I scratched the back of my head. She didn't answer.

"I guess even you have to get tired sometime, heh," I chuckled softly.

I sat down in front of her. She foresaw me questioning her action, and so she answered my curiosity with a few more hand gestures. She raised her arm to the sky, and then closed her eyes for a few moments before opening them again to look at me.

"T-Tomorrow?" I asked her with a squint. She gazed into my eyes for a few moments before shutting hers, this time without reopening them. Her triangle began to dimly glow in the darkness of the night as she relaxed her posture. I figured it might have been their way of sleeping, or perhaps meditating. Either way, I figured I should also get some rest. I brushed off the area within a few square feet of me. I lay on my side with my arm tucked under my face and peeked over at her once more. She looked so regal just sitting there.

"What can be going through her mind? What are her intentions? Why did she bring me here?" The thoughts beamed around my fatigued cranium and everything within it.

Her aura filled the area with a violet light, preventing me from falling asleep for a while. I didn't mind. Watching her live in such peace was mesmerizing. All I could do was gaze at her while I *p*ondered what life had thrown at me in such a short time.

My exhaustion was being rewarded as I drifted away. Tomorrow held many possible outcomes, many possible dangers. I hopped it didn't serve up the latter.

CHAPTER 6

The Eye

I woke up feeling surprisingly refreshed. Especially after sleeping on some damn rocks. The moment I opened my eyes, I felt a surge of purely invigorating clean energy. I looked around for the being. She stood up straight and stared out into the eyes of the city. I could feel the sense of longing she possessed.

"Has she been there before?" I questioned.

I rose rather quickly to my feet in excitement. I was curious about the wonders lying within the mysterious crystal city. The being didn't look back at me, but the moment she heard the dirt rustle below my shoes, she began walking down the path. I made sure to keep up with her. The city looked extremely close by. Yet, somewhat like a cloud, it was far more distant than I had expected. We walked together for about an hour on a straight path.

Even in the daylight, the city was a sight to see. The closer we got to it, the more of the colorful trees we found; and when we got within a mile, we began to find the crystals. They shined brightly in the sun's light, partially distracting me from the road ahead. Within minutes, I noticed we encountered crystals that were larger and larger until one about half my size caught my eye specifically. Its reflection and intrigue wouldn't let me go anywhere else without first inspecting it.

I got closer to the being and said softly, "Hey ... uh ... wait a second. I want to ... check this out."

She stopped walking, turned her whole body around, and looked me in the eyes again. After a few seconds, she walked over to the crystal and put her hand directly on the tip of it. I followed her. The crystals in plain sight were all in bunches and grew directly out of the ground similar to stalagmites. Yet unlike normal stalagmites, these crystals were much wider and were geometrically formed with a point at the top. They looked like clear quartz.

I squatted down to get an eye-level view. They were nearly transparent, and remarkably so. I couldn't explain why, but I decided to press my palms directly to it. Immediately, I felt a flow of energy through my hands fueling me with clarity and insightful thoughts. My eyes widened, and I took a deep inhalation.

"What is this? This is amazing!" I yelled with glee. I smiled and almost laughed uncontrollably. She was closing her eyes once more, and the purple triangle, as expected by this time, began to shine brightly.

I stood up from my squat without letting my hands leave the crystal. I moved my face closer and looked within it. It reminded me of something, yet I couldn't wrap my head around what exactly. I progressively inched in closer and closer until my warm breath formed a circle of condensation on its surface. The clairvoyance and level of intensity heightened as my heart raced.

I broke into a sweat. My pupils dilated. The grainy sand and dirt below swirled around us without touching our skin. It was as if our auras lifted them purely with energetic force. I felt a slow hum of vibration in my heart beginning to spread throughout my entire body.

"I can't believe this right now! I'm without words! Do you feel what I feel—uh . . . I'm still not sure what to call you . . . but this is incredible!" I yelled in joy. A few moments of wild smiling and uncommon facial expressions later, the unexpected happened once more. Considering the words that had just left my lips, irony shot through my perception like an arrow of astonishment.

Slowly and with a soft grumble, I heard something coming from the being. All other feelings and thoughts ceased in light of the sound. I moved my face away from the crystal and, in near disbelief, turned my eyes over to her. The sand and dirt had stopped moving yet was still in mid-air. She had her palm firmly placed onto the crystal. The grumble became clearer after every attempt until the suspense was broken.

"Leira . . . I am Leira." My jaw dropped in awe. She spoke to me. I let out the breath I had been holding the entire time.

"This is real. This is all real. You just said something! In my language!" I was vociferating at this point. I dug deeper through my mind.

"She claimed identity through a name! Had she been given the name before? Can't be. She didn't have my language to provide her with the combination of sounds. She must have crafted this in a day's time! How is this possible?" I was conversing with myself. I shook my head in half-enlightened bewilderment.

"But then again, at this point, anything should be in realm of what's possible, huh, Sam?" I had considered that maybe she could or had the ability to speak, yet I doubted the probability of it actually happening. But here I was, in the presence of a being with the capabilities to learn a language in a single day, at least a name. It took my breath away, and for a while I was left ironically speechless.

She kneeled down and plucked one of the crystals a few inches in length out of the ground. The moment it left the planet's surface, it shined a deep, fluorescent indigo and then quickly returned to quartz-like transparency. She made another grumble, but this time only for a moment.

"Come," she said as she outstretched her fist to me. She opened her hand with the crystal sitting on her palm as if she wanted me to take it from her. I wanted to grab it, but I was as frozen as the floating dirt and rocks were. She smiled, reached down to my right hand, put the crystal in the center of my palm, and then closed my fingers around it. Smiling again, she took a step back to face the city.

I blinked a few times, shrugging off my brain's runaway train of thoughts. I finally let go of the large crystal, but traces of the feeling remained. The small one, huh? A low hiss signaled the sand and gravel falling. I looked down at the crystal in my hand. Whatever it was, it held some sort of power I knew I might use again. I put it into the pocket of my near skin-tight jumpsuit and focused my attention back on the city.

A few hundred feet before reaching the entrance, I started finding it difficult to breathe. My chest became heavy, and I felt weaker. Almost as if gravity itself was being altered. I took a few long breaths while at the same time losing the pace with "Leira." She noticed me falling behind, and so she stopped and pointed to my pocket.

Without thinking twice, I reached back into my pocket and gripped it tightly. As I regained my strength, my breathing went back to normal.

"Why does the crystal help me? And why do I feel this way as we get closer to the city?" I was still a bit hesitant to speak to her in a fluent manner, but I had to ask anyway.

She replied after a small, petite grumble. "Crystal help you. Feel like us." She could only speak in small fragments, but I was still amazed by her ability.

"Okay. Thank you, Leira," I replied with a thin smirk. It was my first time saying her name. It sounded nice. Saying it felt like home; it rolled off the tongue. She smiled back and kept walking toward the city.

Within minutes, we arrived at the first set of pyramids. We strolled down a lane, passing by the first two pyramids. I assumed the entryways all faced the larger pyramid; therefore, I would have to hang a right at the first four-way intersection to see the being living inside.

"There's no way that . . . other being . . . got to them first, right?" I wondered.

The second I turned to head toward the entrance, I felt Leira's hand on my shoulder. I shot her a confused glance.

"Come," she spoke without as much grumbling this time. The words sounded more clear and confident. Her hand left my shoulder. She pointed to the larger pyramid as she began walking in its direction. I simply nodded. She began walking once again. I followed, looking back at the pyramids we passed.

There were indeed beings inside. Only they were meditating. As she did when she slept.

Every time we passed one of the colorful trees, it glowed as it had before on the ridge. Now, almost always reflecting their light on the crystals around them, creating beautiful illuminations of light. Spectrums of color, with a variety of different shades of red, green, and violet, shined on the walls of nearby moss-lined pyramids and the ground below as well.

Before long, I found myself staring face-to-face with one of the largest structures I had ever seen. The closer we got to the monumental pyramid, the more I realized how truly massive it was. *"How did they construct such a colossal building?"* I pondered.

Several times larger than the ruins of the Great Pyramids of Giza, the titanic collection of stone towered over the city. The entrance had a height and shape identical to the smaller pyramids, but of course much larger; relative to its size. Prior to entering, I gazed around the surrounding area for anything new. I predicted I would see a being walking around last minute, but there was still no one. Instead, I looked back at the main pyramid and noticed something peculiar. All of the pyramids were perfectly white; this I knew to be true. Despite all of the clear examples of it, my eyes happened to catch something that would change that truth. At the very top of the grand pyramid, I saw a smudge of color with a general form to it. It wasn't an accident. It looked like something definite was inscribed or drawn up there. The smudge, being too far away for me to decipher, temporarily left my mind.

We were within a few feet from the opening when I found two of the trees with red circular leaves perfectly distant from one another while also being perfectly distant from the corners of the entrance.

"Eat," said Leira as she reached out and plucked off one of the star-shaped fruit.

I remembered I had missed what would have been breakfast, and that I was beginning to feel as cold as when I had first arrived. I snapped a fruit off and again felt the hum through my body. It was ... soothing. It brought me back to the feeling you get moments before you dig into a long-awaited dinner. I threw the fruit into my mouth and chewed past the tarty thrashing it unleashed until it was easy to swallow. I took a deep breath and then looked over at Leira. She had already been looking at me; waiting for me to finish eating. I peered into the dark void past the entrance.

"How are we going to see inside of there?" I asked.

She slowly walked backward into the pyramid as she spoke, triangular marking shining brightly.

"Many trees inside. Light path to The Eye." I raised my eyebrows.

"The Eye? What is that exactly? What does it mean?" Her gaze was deeply locked onto mine. Almost uncomfortably so.

"God," she said, simple significance. Chills made their way through my whole body. She continued walking backward, revealing the glowing trees. They illuminated the inside of the pyramid; just enough to show they lined a pathway to something in the distance.

"Wait . . . what?" I had never truly believed in God, but I was also past the realm of full-on disbelief on anything at this point.

We kept pressing forward without a word. My anxiety flared. I pushed my hair back and choppily let out a delayed exhale. I squinted in front of me. I could barely make out about a hundred meters ahead of us. Yet I could see a ring of the trees glowing dimly with three small pyramids within it and a crystalline shape in the center of them. It floated perfectly still and had the shape of a Merkaba just as the fruit was. I had read about the shape once. Many people believed it held a way to contact beings of higher power. I usually kept an open mind about beliefs and practices, but never gave a genuine second thought about it. Until now.

As we got closer, I noticed something engraved or written on different parts of it, but I couldn't make them out. Leira's triangular marking began to shine brighter and brighter. I spoke up.

"Leira. What do you mean by God?" She answered without looking back at me, still walking.

"The Eye is not A God. We are God. I is We, and The is Me. We are together God. The Eye gives this power." She hadn't grumbled at all before speaking. And her speech felt eerily refined. I didn't know what to say. We just kept walking until we were right in front of it.

We came to a stop, and the trees started to glow brighter than I had seen them glow before. The Merkaba, one great chunk of what appeared to be polished crystal, hovered in midair without moving.

Suddenly, the massive crystal began to spin. The speed picked up, faster and faster. The wind whirled, slicing through the air. Its terrifying sound echoed powerfully through the entire pyramid. Within a few moments of reaching top speed, an image projected directly from the face of it. It looked nearly holographic and somewhat translucent, as if it was an independent image altogether. It was an eye. Not *their* eye, but **my** eye. A **human** eye. It stared into my soul. Pierced me with ambiguous intensity. A mysterious wave of intrigue filled me. I was being drawn to it. But . . . I was terrified.

I turned to look at Leira. "Leira... What's . . . going on?" I asked firmly, my speech weakening as I let out the last couple of words. She pointed at her purple triangle and then walked closer to me.

Gently, she touched my forehead and said, "You are also God. You just don't know it yet."

I didn't know what to make of this new information that I was given. The mighty crystal whizzed faster and faster only serving to make me more uncomfortable.

"What . . . the hell does she mean by that? What do we do here, Sam?" I wondered worriedly. I was infinitely curious as to why the three-dimensional eye on the Merkaba was a human looking one. *"Have they encountered a human before? How?"* I considered. I glanced back behind me at the empty black abyss the trees' light couldn't reach. Leira's voice pulled me back.

"You must become one." Her speech was getting more clearly pitched by the moment. She continued.

"We all become one."

"How do I do that? Should I . . . do that?" I asked under my breath. Leira nodded.

"You must." I took a step back.

"Will I still be *me?*" I questioned myself aloud. Leira approached the spinning crystal and raised her hand to it. Before she got within a meter or two, it began to repel her as if a magnet tried forcing the same charges to collide.

Leira brandished a slightly dissatisfied expression; one I hadn't seen her make.

"This Eye rejects me. It hungers for you." Her face read a fierce determination.

*"**This** eye?"* I thought.

I wondered if I even had a choice as whether or not to "become one" with it. Could I back out now? Turn around and walk away? I took a step back but then began to feel a subtle gravitational pull toward the crystal. I was being invited. I looked again, deeply and directly, into the Eye. I swallowed in involuntary nervousness. It was then I decided.

I balled my fists and approached the violently spinning crystal.

I knew that if I got too close, the sharp edges of the Merkaba would instantly shred my hands to pieces. I walked gingerly in a straight line directly in front of it. Its eyelid was a little more than halfway opened, as if it barely cared about me being here. Yet somehow, I could feel that was far from the truth.

The closer I got, the more drawn to it I felt; not mentally, but physically. My feet began to slide on the dirt and sand beneath me. I gulped a long gulp and raised my shaking hands toward it. Once I was around a few meters away, the pull was strong enough to slowly drag me toward it without having to lean forward or move at all.

I broke into a nervous sweat trickling quickly down my face. The moment the sweat fell from my chin, it split off and was sucked into the psychic pull of the crystal.

I started to breathe heavily through my nose. Before I knew it, I was off my feet and moving diagonally toward it. The

Merkaba, being nearly twelve feet off of the ground, caused me to glide through the air completely. From my vantage point, I noticed a large, pitch-black pool of water in the distance. My concentration on it was quickly broken as I became dangerously close to the Eye. I rose to it, realizing there was no turning back. I lowered my arms back down, squinted, and turned my head away.

"Embrace it," Leira's soft voice emanated from below. A few moments later, my speed accelerated, and I was hurled forward. I gritted my teeth in preparation but then realized I had stopped moving and was simply hovering. The hissing sound came to an immediate stop as well.

My sight being blurry for a moment, returned to see an empty white void. The Eye, only a foot or two away, stared through me. It flickered in and out of visibility. Its eyelid blinked within the hologram, as a real eye would. The crystal behind it was slowing to a halt. After ten seconds of the Eye fluctuating in and out of complete transparency, it vanished altogether. The Merkaba itself, now completely still, radiated waves of energy through my body.

I felt a curious tickle on my forehead and smaller ones elsewhere around my body. I looked down at a small scar on my hand. It was being smoothed over. Erased. As if it never happened. Other imperfections followed.

This was the moment I was supposed to touch it. I just *knew*. I raised my arms once again and rested my palms on the surface of the Merkaba. I was instantly faced with the same sensations I had when I touched the first crystal just outside the city. Feelings of enlightenment and purity raced through the tracks of my mind. I felt as though I was being unlocked; like I had been limited my entire life.

A faint, violet glow formed around my body. My skin's imperfections had all been completely filled in like cracks in a sidewalk. Everything felt so right and just . . . correct for once.

Just then, the very essence of my being was extracted and flew into the Merkaba. Frequencies of unknown origin interweaved with what I could only describe as my soul. I had no control. And perhaps I was never meant to have it in the first place. What even was I? What even am I? What is "I?" What? I couldn't even begin to quantify the length of time I spent marveling underneath the layers of my perception within the crystal. I could have been there for minutes, hours, or even days, and it would have not made a difference whatsoever, nor would I be able to quantify the length with any semblance of accuracy anyways.

A vision flooded my consciousness. I saw a visibly older being walk into the black pool behind the Merkaba. Moments later, two beings arose, brand new. The same, but different. *Reborn into two beings.* I then saw the planting of the colorful trees by slightly more humanoid looking beings. I saw great power being wielded. Mass consumption of the fruit, the building of the pyramids through psychic powers. The death of many trees. And the deaths of many beings. The vision showed me two older beings going into the pool this time. And two new ones arising from the pool.

"What . . . does this all mean?" I questioned mentally. The thoughts echoed audibly in my psyche. I could hear them aloud.

A final series of visions flashed swiftly. I saw me. I faded and then saw the first being I had interacted with on the planet. He faded too. Then, what looked like a hand encased in crystalized armor reach up to a Merkaba; like the one I just had. They were quickly swallowed up by it. And then I felt vibrations of the planet from within the vision. Destruction. Cataclysm.

Suddenly, my body felt cold and my surroundings dark. The feeling was almost unfamiliar to me. As if I hadn't felt something tactile in a long while. In the space of two seconds, I was thrust back into reality.

CHAPTER 7

The Rebirth

I came to, in what felt like a bottomless pit of murky water. It was absolutely freezing. I desperately swam to the surface, taking in a huge breath. I coughed a few times while swimming in any direction I could. My vision was blurry and slow to return to normal.

I reached the edge of the pool and just barely managed to hoist myself out in a few tries. While opening and closing my eyes simultaneously, I came to the realization I had been in the black pool behind the Merkaba.

"Reborn?" I wondered.

As I began walking toward the other side of the crystal, I noticed I was outlined with a lavender glow. I looked down at my palms and then at my knuckles and veins. Leira caught my attention. I turned to her as she peered up at me from a meditative pose.

"How do you feel?" she asked. But I couldn't speak yet. I was lost in awe and was unable find a way to articulate what I had been feeling. I couldn't quite say what I wanted to. But I felt utterly compelled to.... And without hesitation and pure impulsivity, I reached for and touched her purple triangle with my index finger. Within seconds, I began to hear a voice within my head.

"So you understand now?" she asked with a long, trailing echo. My eardrums vibrated in unison, and it tickled a bit.

My eyes widened. "Leira?" I asked while shooting her a confused look. She nodded her head gently and smiled.

"So is it telepathy? A way of communicating?"

"Much more than that. It's a way to completely understand each other. You will begin to interpret feelings and emotions among other things as you undergo changes," she replied. I took a step back, lowering my hand from her triangle and looked up into her eyes

"Changes? What . . . kind of changes?" There was a bit of hesitation on the edge of my lips, yet it felt wrong to be hesitant.

"Do I really want to know?" I questioned myself. *"This could be the first step towards 'becoming a God' like she said. But do I even want to become a God in the first place? What does that even mean? I still don't know."*

"That is to be understood with time, Samuel. Everything changes at different points in time. Understanding the true importance of embracing it is a journey within a journey," she stated with a serious undertone and then paused. She began again.

"Now, you'll do what you're meant to do." I squinted in confusion.

"What am I meant to do? I don't know what that even is. Here . . . or anywhere else. . . ."

"But you will," she responded softly. I lowered my finger from her marking and looked into her eyes.

"It's amazing how well you can communicate . . . considering you just learned my language, like, yesterday." I smirked.

"All that you know, I know. When we first touched, everything became more and more clear with time." I retreated into troubling thoughts.

"Does that mean . . ."

"Yes, it means that *he* too knows all that you know," she replied with a minuscule yet identifiable sense of dissatisfaction. I stared at her for a moment before responding. I was amazed at her sudden ability to speak so eloquently. It was apparent that during my time in the Merkaba, I wasn't the only one who had changed. I shook off the distraction and returned to the present moment.

"Well. Why did you two react so differently? Why did he . . . attack those people?" Before she could answer, I added more with a shred of hesitation; still shaken up by recalling it.

"I think I saw him in the vision. When I was up there. I saw somebody reach out to the Eye. But then . . . destruction."

"Destruction?"

"Yeah. Trust me, I know what it looks like. . . . What does he want? What could he want?"

She answered swiftly, as if she had been thinking about the thought long before I triggered a reason to express it.

"We were without desire before you. All we were created to do was become one with the Eye, consume, and reproduce. Before you. Before you *imprinted* on us. With him, through fear," I didn't like that word. "Imprinted." I looked down, no doubt guided by a repressed sense of shame.

"I guess it doesn't matter what planet I'm on then. . . ." Leira sensed my feelings.

"You did not know." I fell silent for a moment before responding.

"Well, what do we do now?" Leira looked as though she had been waiting for me to ask.

"We—" but just before she could answer fully, I dropped to a knee in a daze. My body seemed to bottom out in fatigue all at once. I realized I must have been inside the Merkaba for a lengthy period of time.

Leira went to a tree and snapped two fruits off. She handed them both to me.

"Two?"

"This time, yes." I nodded and devoured them both quickly. While still chewing, I peered out to the entrance.

"You know . . . maybe if I can just find a way to talk to him . . . the first being . . . maybe I can somehow undo this . . .," I said nearly under my breath.

Leira paused for a moment, no doubt judging the decision before nodding. My deeper thoughts and interpretations of that nod were broken by my damn-near alarming sense of invigoration.

"Whoa! I feel incredible! Twice as strong as before." Leira nodded again. I glanced over at the trees before we started walking back toward the entrance.

"When I was in the Merkaba . . . I saw visions."

"The ancestor's knowledge is always given by the Eye."

"But who are . . . were the ancestors? Why is the Eye shaped like mine?"

"The visions only give what you're meant to see." As a man who liked getting answers to questions, I didn't care for that response, but halfway accepted it.

"Why did the Merkaba choose to show me death then? I saw . . . a lot of dead beings. And dead trees."

"This is why only this time you eat two."

"Right," I replied with a swift exhale. I continued again.

"Well, if there weren't enough fruit to go around, then why not just plant new trees?"

"They take five-hundred years to grow. If we ate more than we need . . . we'd go—"

"Extinct," I finished her sentence, my eyes widening a bit. Well, that answered that.

"Is that why you, uh . . . only revive yourselves when you get old? Instead of making more of you?" I asked.

"Revive?"

"Yeah . . . from the black pool?" I pointed behind us.

"That is not revival. That is death."

"Death?? But I—"

"Death and then rebirth. Of new beings. Using the Eye, we make newer, younger beings with the originals dying."

"How morbid," I thought. She continued as if she had read my mind.

"It's to not over deplete the world of the fruit. The fruit brings life."

"Heh. A fruit of life. A "**LifeFruit**." I chuckled softly. I spoke up again.

"But these new beings . . . are they . . . you?"

"They are not 'us.' Yet, they are. Just like your children *would* have—" I darted my eyes in her direction.

"I'm . . . sorry." Leira said quietly. I took a moment to reflect.

"You really read my entire mind, didn't you? With just a single touch." Leira looked away, embarrassed. Another new emotion.

"Hey, uh. It's alright. . . ." Before I could think of something else to say, we heard a rustling of feet toward the entrance of the grand pyramid. We both peered out. It was a mass of beings starting to collect there. I felt a tingle on my forehead and reached for it.

"You think they're friendly . . . ?" I questioned, heart rate increasing.

"Only one way to find out. Let us go," she replied with half squinted eyes.

Journal Entry #503

Mom is going to flip when she finds out I dropped out of school. I don't know how much longer I can keep up the "school is great!" talks. Roger is a genius and can always do whatever he wants. But I'm following my dream. And Roger is too. We both want the same thing. I just need to devote more time in order for that to happen. This could be big. He says he's on the verge of a breakthrough and that I could help by getting investors to believe in him. This is where I shine. Where he doesn't. I'm good at talking to people. I'm good at making people believe in this. We can't be the only guys in the world trying to save it. Trying to help it. I'm going to find those people, and they're *going* to fund his research. I'll make sure of it.

THE FEARLESS EYE

CHAPTER 8

The Resistance

We drew closer and closer to the entrance of what I had been mentally calling the "Grand Pyramid." The beings all stood still. Just watching. Staring. I noticed something strange. My body felt . . . different. I stood upright and I breathed far easier than I was used to. I always had mild allergies, preventing me from breathing perfectly; with my poor sight and my slightly congested sense of smell, you'd think I would gather enough power in my other senses to compensate for the lacking, yet of course, that wasn't the case. Instead, I seemed to have decent hearing at best and a fairly normal sense of taste. Lucky me.

I rubbed my hands together as if I was washing them. I looked down at my fingers and found I also wasn't shaking. For the first time in a long, long while, my hands completely still.

I didn't understand why all of these enhancements decided to hit me at once.

"Was it the double dosage of fruit from the . . . 'LifeTree?' Or the crystal?" The thought brought me to realize I no longer held the crystal from outside of the city. Before I had fused with the Merkaba, I had put it in my pocket, where it had remained. I felt great, if not better than ever, and I wasn't holding the crystal in my hand.

I grabbed the crystal out of my pocket and gripped it tightly to compare the difference. Nothing I could make out. I raised it up a bit above eye level and inspected it. It reflected the faint glow of the LifeTrees we passed in a brilliant shine of the uncommon colors. The light emitting from the crystal's surface brought me back to when I first saw the city from the ridge. A sort of subconscious hope lived within the memory of that moment, and I knew I could revisit it anytime I felt I needed to.

I looked up at the beings out front. We had been getting closer, and I still didn't know what I would do about them.

The closer I got, the more strongly I felt their collective presence. I turned to Leira.

"I think they know we're here. They've been waiting for us." She nodded in agreement.

"Yes. I just hope they haven't been affected. It is partly for this possibility that I took you to the Main Pyramid first. The knowledge and power you have now, might just be enough to revert beings that were recently affected." I started to think harder about the situation and then spoke up.

"If these beings are ... infected ... with fear already, there's a chance things could get ... violent. And we'll be outnumbered," I said with thinly lined franticness. I tried not to panic. I considered the variables.

The moment I consciously decided to truly focus, I felt a shift in my brain. My thought process became cleaner and more precise. I thought of possible scenarios quicker than I normally would have. I figured if all beings on the planet were as wise and intelligent as Leira, and if they were hostile, they would have most likely hid their presence until we got outside and then struck. But since they were just stagnantly grouped together, I assumed they were similar to Leira when she had first noticed my presence; they were just curious. Blank slates. I nodded at Leira to show it was okay, and we kept onward.

When we reached the entrance, I realized just how many of the beings were actually there. It appeared to be the entire city gathered in front of the Main Pyramid. All of the beings stood in perfect alignment with identical posture; a good sign.

I let out a sigh of relief and wiped the small bit sweat off of my forehead.

"Whenever you're ready," Leira slipped out smoothly. I was mildly confused but began to understand after a moment or two of thought.

"You mean . . . for me to turn them? Like I did you?" Leira nodded with a smile. I would have loved to focus on how oddly attractive that was, but before I could, one of the beings approached me. He stuck out his finger in an attempt to touch the center of my forehead as Leira and the first being had done. By then I understood the process well and accepted his invitation. With all of the new power and knowledge I had mysteriously gained from the Merkaba, I reached out and did the same for him; sparking the glow of his purple triangle.

After he became enlightened, I realized I had seen the first being spread the fear by having other beings infect each other. I assumed it would also work with the spread of whatever it was I spread. With this realization intact, I attempted to telepathically communicate with him as I did with Leira. I put my finger on his triangle and began to form words out of pure feeling.

But before I could finish a sentence, I felt a headache coming on. I clutched the temple on the left side of my head and tried to massage it. In a matter of moments, the headache grew into what felt like a furious vice grip on my throbbing neurons. I released my telepathy and squinted my eyes. As the pain worsened, I gritted my teeth and fell to my knees.

Leira kneeled down and asked, "Are you ok? What are you feeling?" I wanted to answer her, but the pain was severe enough to prevent me from focusing on speech at all. My nose began to bleed. A loud ringing sounded in my ears. I grabbed at my forehead and growled in pain. I felt as if the very blood circulating through the veins around my skull was magma. Suddenly, I heard a wicked whisper crawl its way into my head.

"Samuel." My eyes blasted open as wide as they could go, before being forced closed.

I re-opened them, only to realize it wasn't my eyes I saw from. It was a vision. From the perspective of . . . the first being I had encountered.

I saw the moment the being struck the other one in the smaller village as if I was doing it myself. I *felt* what the being telepathically communicated to the others with an invective sense of demeaning grandiosity laced within. I heard another whisper from the being.

"What *am I?*" The voiced echoed for a moment before the vision transformed, sending me to another place. A mountain pass.

A reddish-tinted purple light from the being's triangular marking reflected onto the face of a cowering being as it was struck repeatedly. Crystals begin to form around the aggressor's arm. ~~My arm~~ . . . the first being's arm. He was being completely encased in a crystal mold. But it wasn't hostile. It was what he wanted. A growth of power. A symbiosis with the nature of the planet. What the ancestors of these people had used. The voice spoke again into my ears.

"*Who* am I?" The trailing words thrust me into another vision. This time a forest. A forest of dead, decaying trees.

I saw through his eyes as he looked down at his hands. Darkened crystal gauntlets surrounded his greyed fingertips. Indigo sap fell from them freely. He had just consumed a LifeFruit. Another. And another. Ravenously.

The sound of a large group of people marched behind him. Sounded like . . . an army. He looked over his shoulder and saw many barren LifeTrees, no longer glowing.

"Leumas," he said confidently, no longer in a whisper. He had birthed a name. As Leira had.

The vision shot me deeper into that forest of dead trees; only the dark of night enveloped the surroundings like an ominous blanket.

A triangular marking, many times larger than a normal one, glowed a pale white, piercing the hazy darkness. The voice—Leumas's voice—spoke once more.

"Rise."

Thunderous steps boomed closer and closer before its source let out a vicious and terrifying roar.

The sheer power of the sound shocked me completely out of the trance. The vision subsided. The pain slowly slithered its way out of the veins encasing my head.

Leira's shouts for me were muffled behind the ringing slowly beginning to fade. She touched my forehead and then took a nervous step back. She spoke to me telepathically.

"That was him, wasn't it?" I nodded in confirmation before speaking up in a tired rasp.

"He's got an army. He's . . . eating all of the fruit. . . . I just don't kn—"

"How about you start by getting up and looking at what's in front of you?" Leira interrupted firmly.

I struggled to my feet and peered out at the massive crowd of beings. My thoughts echoed loudly in my head.

*"It's either I... awaken them, or Leumas does. This.... is how I stop him. And I **need**, to stop him. Who knows what will happen to this planet if I don't? You saw what you saw in that vision Sam..."* I conversed with myself mentally. Leira was glancing in my direction. I looked into her eyes as she spoke up again.

"You've always put the world before everything else in your life. Haven't you?" I didn't know how to answer that. She stared at me with ambiguous eyes.

"Yeah . . . I have," I responded softly.

"Well, I don't expect that you'll be stopping now. Will you?" Leira said, knowing what my answer would be. I took a moment before taking in a deep breath, exhaling more confidently.

"No. I won't." The wind blew the hair back out of my face.

I made my way back over to that first being. I touched his forehead as it touched mine. The being was fully awakened, just as Leira was.

I nodded and looked back out at the crowd in its entirety. "Alright. Who's next?" I asked with new purpose.

CHAPTER 9

The Ascension

After a healthy amount of teamwork and forehead touching, hundreds of beings were blank slates no longer. I put my hands on my hips as I watched the beings mingle with each other. The games of charades led to much understanding and a lot of bright, shining triangles.

Seeing the early stages of their communication placed a smirk on my face. It reminded me of when I had first met Leira. Looking back made it feel like I had met her a week or two before; yet, if I didn't count my time in the Merkaba, it had only been a single day.

The sky darkened around the edges as the sun began to set. Naturally, following such a mentally and physically draining day, it was time for some serious rest. My body... (soul?) clamored for it. I needed it; somehow, I just knew. If I had to raise my arm one more time, my shoulder would cramp up and spaz out on me.

The dirt and rocks a few feet away had my name on it. But just as I knelt down, I felt a hand grab my elbow. I looked back over my shoulder and saw a being standing before me. I could feel a peculiar bit of energy leading me to believe it was the first one from the city I had enlightened. He half-smiled and awkwardly waved in an attempt to ask me to go somewhere with him.

I let out a puzzled sigh. I was crashing, not really feeling like going anywhere with anyone. And yet, I didn't want to stifle the being's gesture.

"You're the first being I met here, aren't you?" The being nodded silently.

"Too early for language, huh?" I wondered.

I peered out in search of Leira. Found her working with some of the newer beings. Talking to them, no doubt trying to help them along on their learning process. Our eyes met. I called her over. She finished up and approached us.

"What's going on?" she asked simply.

"He wants me to go with him somewhere. Wanna come?" Leira first looked at the stoic being, then at me once more. A smile was painted onto her face as she nodded.

"Good. Well, uh . . . let us go," I said with a hand motion.

The other being hesitated before moving. He looked deeply into the Leira's eyes. He then got within arm's reach and extended his finger to her triangle. But just before he could touch it, she swiftly grabbed his hand. I was a little stunned, not sure how to read that.

"Shouldn't you be practicing your speech instead?" she asked plainly.

The being's expression went from stoic to minutely sour. He withdrew his hand slowly and waved for us to follow him. Leira shot me a glance, uncovering my nervous, awkward-sourced smile.

We walked down the path through one of the city's lanes in complete silence. After ten minutes or so, we reached a pyramid. Seemed like it was *his* pyramid.

I peered inside. It seemed even larger on the inside than it did on the outside. Roughly, it had the dimensions of a three-story house, as I thought before, but without any additional walls within it. All of that space seemed incredibly pointless for a single being to have. The interior contained nothing but an assortment of small crystals just lying on the floor around what appeared to be an upside-down pyramid with the tip shoved into the dirt. The base of it, exposed to our sight, probably had a four-by-four meter length and width. I wondered if that's where they meditated. It couldn't be any other place.

"I'm guessing all other pyramids look identical on the inside as well." Leira and the being looked at each other for a moment. They looked back at me and nodded their heads. I imagined it was the first time either one of them had been in any pyramid other than their own since birth.

I took a few more steps inside and looked around until I noticed something as I gazed up at the ceiling. The very tip of the pyramid was nearly transparent, bathing the interior in moonlight. It reminded me of a skylight. The ones some houses had in them years ago; before they became a liability instead of a luxury.

"But how did I not notice the clarity of the tips when I was outside?" I wondered. Leira's voice was heard in my head.

"The ancestors made them to protect us from our 'sun.' Because we spend 90 percent of our lives in the same spot, getting too much exposure could shorten our life." I smirked, shielding myself from unpleasant memories I knew they had both seen.

"Not a bad move," I replied quietly, looking back up at the skylight.

I walked over to the inverse pyramid shoved neatly in the ground and brushed my fingertips along the sides. I circled around it, inspecting its details.

Leira's triangular marking began to shine. It drew my attention.

"How about T... trrr... eye? **Treye?**" I questioned, pointing to Leira's marking. Leira touched her forehead for a moment before nodding silently with a small smile. Suddenly, a male voice was heard.

"Goodnight," the being said politely without a grumble. I clapped a couple of times in surprise.

"Wow. Already with language. And understanding cultural stuff like saying goodnight. You're a fast learner... uh..." I searched for a name I knew he hadn't told me. He surprised me yet again with a quick response.

"Regor." My eyes widened a bit.

"Are you... letting us stay in here, Regor?" He looked at me, then at Leira, and then back to me before nodding.

"Thank you for that. I appreciate the break from rocks and dirt," I replied slyly. Regor nodded silently with closed eyes, just before exiting the pyramid.

I looked at Leira. She moved her hand over toward the inverse pyramid, signaling for me to hop on. I did in turn (after clearing my throat).

"This is pure stone. No padding up here or anything.... These guys aren't really concerned with comfort I guess," I thought, chuckling to myself. I was about to begin talking when I was cut off by Leira.

"Tonight, we sleep using our... 'Treye.' Not our brain."

*"**Our** Treye?"* I wondered.

"Well, how do we go about doing that?"

"You close your eyes, clear your mind, and feel your intention. Intent to be rested. Intent to understand the world and yourself. This is how we sleep." I marveled at such a thought. I decided to give it a shot, closing my eyes. Leira spoke softly.

"Now. What do you want? What do you desire most?"

"I, uh . . . I want to help this world. I want to stop what I've started here."

"And what do you really want? Above that? What have you *always* wanted?" I squinted my eyes a little in discomfort.

"What do you mean?"

"Only you can answer. Not me." A field of energy formed around me as I concentrated harder.

"What. Do I . . . want? What. Do I . . . want? What. Do I . . . want? What—"

"—do you want, Samuel?" a late-twenties Ariel asked with fervor. The suburban living room held enough tension to make a python look weak. She continued.

"Do you even know what you want? What you *really* want?" Her tone injected me with rage.

"You know what I want, Ariel! I want to make a difference! Make an ACTUAL impact! And YOU'RE trying to stop it all. Trying to GET IN MY WAY!" I slapped a box containing cheap plastic pregnancy tests off of the coffee table.

"I know that you're faking these. You're desperate. Doing anything you can to anchor me here." Her eyes welled with tears.

"You believe what you want to, Sam. . . . Believe it's all a lie," she choked back a sob before continuing.

"Believe I'd become the monster that you'd rather me be. All to make it easier to let go. Easier to justify!"

"I'm doing what's better for the world. Putting it above what I WANT!"

"No Samuel. This *is* what you want. You know there's a real chance to make a difference in other ways. But you'd rather use Roger's tech. The same tech we know might be reengineered to. . . . You *know* what this technology could do. And you also know . . . that . . . th-this is the way for you to been *seen*. For everyone to finally know YOU'VE had an impact. That you were right all along!" My fury was beyond any form of containment. I responded with frigid, unrelenting ferocity.

"Don't you bother calling me again. Or looking for me. What I'm doing is more important than anything else. More than a simple life. More than a family. And more than **you**." Ariel was taken aback but immediately forced herself to accept it.

"And yet, nothing is ever more important than **you**." The once-repressed tear slid down her cheek, impossible to be held in any longer. I looked at her once more, my convictions reverberating from feeling sound to crumbling and back again. I settled on the decision.

"Goodbye." The words echoed as if they were in my head. Louder and louder they rose in volume, bouncing off the walls of my psyche.

Goodbye.

GoodBYE.

GOODBYE.

GOODBYE!

Good—

"—morning," Leira said calmly, easing me back to reality.

CHAPTER 10

The Five

I didn't know for sure if I had just meditated pretty damn hard or if I actually fell asleep while sitting upright. I opened my eyes and noticed it was still dark outside. I tried to distract myself from the residual effect the dream-memory of my fight with Ariel had on me.

"Morning . . . ? What time is it?" I asked. Leira responded, sounding entirely human.

"Well, I don't have a watch, but I'd say somewhere around 7 a.m. Better question is what *day* is it?" I rubbed my eyes in confusion. I looked at Leira, noticing my glasses were off. I grabbed them without issue, and upon putting them on, they barely enhanced my vision.

"Huh." I looked at Leira. She had a full head of hair and . . . eyelashes. She had developed slightly larger breasts, and her lips had thickened. She even had more of a peach skin tone. I

panned down and noticed she wore *clothes*. A tight piece of clothing covered her entire body with lines in its design all extending from a single triangular marking where the sternum was. Remarkable. I cleared my throat.

"Leira . . . you look . . . different. Um, what the hell happened while I was asleep?" She responded with a smile that extended to her eyes. Even her sclerae were human-like now.

"Well. A lot can happen in a month's time." My mouth dropped.

"A month?!" She nodded, almost laughing. I continued.

"Are you serious? How am I not dead? Starving?! No crick in my neck? Intense lower back pain?! What is going on here?" The laughter escaped her.

"It's normal. The Eye is a lot for any of us to take on. After becoming one with it, we all go into a state of stasis while our Treye fully develops. For you, that took longer than it did for us. But we couldn't wake you until it was over with." I touched my forehead in wild curiosity. Felt nothing unusual. A thought crawled into my head.

"Why didn't she tell me I was going to go into a . . . coma or whatever?" I wondered, mildly disgruntled. She answered as if she had read my mind.

"If I had told you what you were in for, you wouldn't have allowed your mind and spirit to drift." I stared at her. "Fair enough" painted on my face. Suddenly, I *felt* something coming.

As the sun rose behind them, a figure appeared in the doorway, completely silhouetted. Just as before, I just knew that had to be him.

"Regor?" He walked further into the pyramid, revealing himself fully.

"Welcome back, Samuel," he said simply. He approached, seemingly awaiting a reaction.

The closer he got, the more I noticed about his appearance; which was also a complete transformation. He had thick, black hair, similar to my own, with a small bit of wave to it as well. My eyes darted all around Regor from head to toe. He wore a jumpsuit like Leira's, with pockets on the sides and elevated shoulder blade pieces.

"Lots of changes, I see."

Regor smirked. "We all have. Plenty of time for us to evolve while you were in stasis," he replied.

"Evolve?" I thought.

"Well, I guess I've made you all wait long enough."

"Only as long as you needed. But on that note, it's about time we go." I cocked my head a bit.

"Go where? Why so soon?"

"You'll decide that," he responded with certainty as he began walking out. I stopped him.

"Hey, uh. Nice suit. Can I—"

"Of course, Samuel. You think we wouldn't make you one

too? It's not like we were short on time." He smirked as he exited.

I held up my new jumpsuit in awe, admiring the craftsmanship and detailing. I gripped it tightly, running my thumbs over it to feel its texture. It was much thicker and many times more robust than the one I had worn.

"Guess they don't need paper-thin jumpsuits on a planet where their sun won't outright kill them," I thought. Regor spoke up from outside as I changed.

"We like to call them **Perceptive Suits.** I designed them myself," he said proudly.

"What do the hardened triangles on the palms do?" I asked.

"We melted the crystals down to a liquid to form them and used LifeTree bark and sap for the fabric. The triangle on the sternum is the same. They're power amplifiers. When one taps into his or her energy, the amplifiers allow for deeper connections between the suit and the user. This allows the suit to feel and respond to your specific needs. It has a better idea of what you require within any given moment that way." I chuckled at the exposition.

"You make the suit sound like it's alive."

"It is," he replied behind a smile.

"I'll pretend that isn't creepy."

I stepped out into the new sunlight of a departing day. The suit felt . . . good. Like nothing I had ever worn before. Inconceivably incredible. It form-fit to me in every way. Not too tight to become uncomfortable; it was merely an extension of me.

I wiggled my toes inside the built-in boots of the suit. The boots moved around my toes as I did so. Bizarre.

"So you said 'specific needs.' How much variance could the needs of anybody even be?" I asked as three other beings came our way; Leira following behind them. A sarcastic, gruff, yet feminine voice spoke up from the group.

"So that's Samuel. Strange seeing him with . . . new eyes." Her smirk was showcased when her head finally eclipsed the slowly rising sun behind her. Studying her features revealed half of her head was shaved, and the other red hair that reached her shoulder. She had an edgy jawline and piercing spearmint eyes. Her burgundy, skin-tight suit had sharpened crystals poking out of her pocket.

"The name's Sandy," she proclaimed. She seemed unshakable.

"Nice to meet you . . . again?" I chuckled nervously. I looked to her right. There stood a muscular being with his arms crossed. He had short, dark-brown hair and sported well-kept facial hair. His midnight-blue suit had the indents outlining his muscles' separation. He had a thick strap across his chest, no doubt holding onto some weapon on his back, and he also had crystal casings around his knuckles. Definitely had an intimidating presence about him.

"And what's your na—"

"Buster," he interrupted, shooting a bit of a glare my way. Sandy spoke up.

"C'mon now, Buster! Lighten up! He *did* make us who we are," she said with another smirk framing her tone. I put my hand on my chin. Pondered for a moment.

"What exactly do they mean? What strange corner of my brain did these two sprout from?"

Regor cleared his throat, likely trying to put ease to the awkward tension.

"And lastly, this is Kobe. He prefers not to speak unless absolutely necessary, and we have agreed not to force him to." I glanced over at Kobe's facial expression. It hadn't changed since the moment they had arrived. He had a straight, black, bowl-cut and his eyes hid behind thick black goggles. His jumper was completely black and was by far the most plain. Regor spoke up.

"They received a bit of an accelerated evolution. Due to being the first three to be connected to you, after contact with the Eye. Besides me of course. Each of them has a unique ability because of this. As do I. And we'll need them." Regor paused for a moment. Leira had shot him a glare she had tried to hide under a layer of stoicism. Regor clearly picked up on it. He continued.

"And we mustn't forget Leira. She's developed an especially helpful ability as well. Now. Come with us. Time to address the others." I raised an eyebrow.

"The others?"

"Yes. The city of course." I nodded nervously. Leira and I exchanged glances. She softened when our eyes met. She spoke up to clarify.

"*It*'s time for you to choose."

CHAPTER 11

The Direction

Regor, Leira, and I followed the others through the city. A swift dagger of chilly wind pierced through me. It prompted the thought I needed a fruit from the LifeTree to bring myself back to comfort.

I found a tree slightly off of the trail. I was being drawn to it. It felt like the immense energy within it called out to me. When my hands made contact with it, my arms became numb from sheer excitement; either that, or it was some sort of chemical reaction from the LifeTree and my suit touching. I plucked off the fruit I desired and my suit vibrated in resonance with the tree's humming. They were in perfect unison. I threw the fruit into my mouth, and enjoyed it more than I had before.

"Considering the fact that I haven't eaten in an entire month . . . 'stasis' or not, my body had to be yearning for something," I thought.

My breathing cleared up, and any hunger or thirst I had vanished. My body slowly warmed to an ideal temperature. I hadn't felt that cold since before entering the city. I rubbed my hands on my arms in an attempt to warm myself up. The new suit felt as if it had even less protection than my original suit did somehow; despite being noticeably thicker. It was like I didn't have clothes on at all. It felt like . . . an extension of my skin. Regor noticed me struggling and laughed with a closed mouth. I saw him smiling in my peripheral vision.

I turned my head to him, smirked, and said, "I see you find my current state humorous." I purposely articulated in the best way I could. His vocabulary and sentence structure rivaled that of my brother's. He paused for a moment and brought his face back to a near emotionless expression.

"With patience comes guidance, Samuel. The suits have the ability to adapt to its user's physical and mental states."

I blankly stared while I waited for him to explain further. I liked the sound of it, but I wasn't sure how it would actually know what state I was in. He pointed at my suit and continued speaking.

"You'll notice the fabric coming to states of transfiguration when conscious thoughts are fed into it, via patches that are connected and streamed through your nervous system on the inside of your suit." I looked down at my right arm and tugged the sleeve outward, rubbing my fingers together. I tried to look for and feel the patches to get an idea of what he talked about, but even then, I didn't quite understand.

"How were you able to create such technology in such a short time?" I asked him. He ignored the question at first.

"Feed your thoughts and intentions into the suit. Tell it that you're cold." My confused glance was replaced by closed eyes as I concentrated. The material and texture of the suit suddenly started vibrating on my hands, feet, groin, and neck area. I paid close attention to the jumper's changes as Regor spoke again, answering my question from before.

"The suit is not as much 'technology' as it is an organism. The LifeTrees began to morph and adapt to the creation process, bending to our will. Engineering at a rapid pace was rather simple; especially considering that we are several times more efficient at storing, processing, and analyzing data than an average human would be." I looked back up at him and tried to ignore the "human" comment.

Within moments, it had formed thicker and warmer protective texture at the extremities, and the purple triangle on my sternum was now a bright red-orange. I looked around at everyone else. Their sternums shined the same color, like if they too had felt cold and desired warmth. I was once again impressed. Regor nodded politely to confirm my statement. The chills I had faded gradually until I was left with a feeling of optimal comfort.

Before long, we reached the edge of the city where the hundreds of other beings had gathered. I peered out into the masses, noticing none of them seemed as far into their transformation as the others, and all of their suits resembled one another's in general appearance, as well as having a similar variety of crystal weapons on their waistlines. It was then I truly understood how special Regor, Leira, and the three others really were.

The group came to a stop a few meters away from the crowd. As soon as the other beings noticed I was in front of them all, they sat down with legs crossed in near unison. Regor walked over to my side.

"Now you must decide what direction to head in," he said plainly. Too plainly.

I peered out at the masses and felt a wave of anxiety wash over me. I had been here before. In a position to make a decision for others. With others relying on me.

"How am I supposed to know where to go?" I replied under my breath.

Regor heard me and replied, "We go North, we head towards the Great Mountain. Home of the other Eye." Leira darted a quick glance in my direction. I only noticed it in the desperate edge of my peripheral.

"Why are there two? Besides... you know... two eyes making sense for us to have." I chuckled nervously and quietly.

"As far as I, and every other being is concerned, it's to maintain equilibrium. Electro-magnetic balance on the planet is controlled by them both." I blinked for a moment, in the darkness of my eyelids, seeing from Leumas's perspective once again. He had been looking up at that very mountain. I just *knew* it.

Regor continued. "We go south instead, we'll find other villages. Other beings to recruit." I squinted a bit.

"Recruit?"

"Yes. Recruit. We'll need all the assistance we can get in our fight against Leumas."

I turned my entire body toward him. "Wait. Fight? Why are we fighting him in the first place? I just want to talk—"

"Don't be naïve, Samuel. Leumas will have not a shred of mercy upon our people. Did you expect us to simply travel unprepared for attack?"

I looked around, again noticing the weapons at the belts of all the citizens.

"I . . . I can't. You said it yourself. Leumas won't have mercy on them. So I shouldn't be leading them. Not to whatever awaits them where he's headed. Where . . . I'm headed."

"They were created in your image . . . by your mind. . . . You must lead them—"

"I didn't-- they were here when I got here. . . . Besides, I don't think . . . I should be leading anybody anyways. . . . I'll head north. Alone."

Regor locked eyes with me. I couldn't tell if they held disappointment, regret, bewilderment, or all of the above. I had no idea. His suit began to vibrate visibly around his neck as he turned around to face the crowd. As he spoke, his voice was amplified outward many times over.

"Crystal City! It's time we move on. There was a monster created amongst our people. A monster that if left unchecked will in fact drain our world of its resources in wake of his own desires. And so we are heading towards the Great Mountain. Where Leumas is. We will face him head on. . . ." Regor's roar lulled as he paused for a moment.

"But we need all of YOU. Every single one of you can all help create a world without fear or oppression. To help undo what has begun here. YOU can aid the change of your planet. YOU can help stop Leumas!" The crowd boomed in collective cheer. He turned to look at me.

"We planned this, Samuel. While you were in stasis, we devised defensive courses of action to be taken on the chance conflict occurs. Sandy's our scout. Kobe's our strategist, and Buster's the muscle. We WILL protect our home. With or *without* you." A voice stepped up in my defense.

"I think you're forgetting who we'll need to deal with Leumas directly. Their minds are connected. We can't do this without Samuel." It was Kobe; the first time he had spoken since I met him. Regor swallowed his words. Sandy spoke up this time.

"Alright, alright. We all want the same thing . . . right? Right?" The crowd of beings still cheering parted down the middle, making a path for us to go through. The group all looked to me for confirmation. I nodded hesitantly.

"Looks like they're not giving me a choice," I thought silently.

Journal Entry #782

Not a day goes by where I don't think of Ariel. And there's not a damn thing I can do about it. No matter who I meet, who I talk to, what I take . . . I can't escape her face. But this . . . this is everything. Nothing can or will eclipse this. The tech Roger created, the materials. He—we—found a way to take the sun's power and really harness it. One-thousand times more efficient than anything before it. Using these solar lasers, we've been able to mine much, much quicker. Cuts right through just about anything. This is an absolute game changer. We'll be going worldwide with this. Give people the help they need.

CHAPTER 12

The Opposition

The group and I made our way through the barren flatland after a few hours of walking. We didn't take a single break. It seemed like they all had our spirits heightened with determination; and it could have been enough to distract them from the fatigue they probably felt.

I was going to spark conversation with Buster and Sandy when I felt a tug from behind me. Leira.

"Hey there," I said behind a smile. She didn't return it.

"Samuel. I've been meaning to ask you something since this morning." I waited with peaked curiosity.

"Go on," I replied.

"Regor and the others planned this. Like he said. With the decision being to give you the choice; as to whether we go towards Leumas or not. I want to know. Is where we're heading really what you want to do? Wouldn't it be easier to let the

115

others handle this? The world handle this? If you wanted, we could simply turn around and just—" I cut her off with a hand on her shoulder.

"No... I have to do this. I made this mess and I've got to be the one to take care of it. And you heard Kobe, I might be the only one who can get through to him." Leira was beginning a retort when I spoke up again.

"I...listen. You've seen what I've done. What became of my world. I just...want to..."

"I know Samuel. I know..." Leira replied, sounding almost disappointed. I was happy to have her caring about my safety, but I never let my own wellbeing stop me from striving towards my goals before, and I wouldn't stop now. *Couldn't* stop now.

I peered over at Regor who walked a little further up in the front. He looked like he was bothered by something.

"Doing alright?" I asked. He replied to me after what seemed like coming back to reality from a daydream.

"Yes, Samuel. I'm fine." An unenthusiastic response; it was expected. I started to introspect about how and why I expected it. My thoughts spiraled a little uncontrollably. My eyes darted around going from Regor, to Leira, to Sandy, to Buster, and then to Kobe, who I didn't speak to but somehow . . . understood.

"*They all just completely formed their personalities from scratch. This much was communicated to me. But was it really from scratch? They all picked my mind clean. And from that, they attached themselves to something. To some . . . piece of me. Their subconscious mind was built upon that. Built upon a mixture of me and whatever they decided to latch onto. They're . . . me. But also, not me. I don't even know how to make heads or tails of it all. It's mind-bending. When I talk to them, it's like talking into a mirror. But only a piece of myself exists in that mirror. Like I'm talking to a fragment; a shard of me. It's . . . bizarre. Bordering on frightening.*" I rubbed my face in apparent awe, blended with an unworldly bewilderment. My thoughts continued.

"*But then again . . . I mean . . . what are humans really? Just a tonic of our parents' chemistry mixed in with society's influences. Many shards and fragments of what we experience. What we invite into our lives. At some level, how are these beings any different from what I am? I was merely influenced and forged my identity based on the collective bits of media and society that I consumed my entire life. And these beings? Just that again, but through me. I'm their TV screen. Their reflection.*" A chill slithered through me as I let out a slow exhale.

I looked out behind me. The mass of beings following the group was an incredible sight. I turned back around only to notice an odd change of scenery in the distance. Reaching the edge of the wasteland brought about the beginning of something new. Every couple of minutes, we would run into a few rotten, decayed, nearly white bushes and trees. Without paying them much mind, I noticed they grew larger in number the further we traveled. We navigated on until it was apparent we were surrounded by them.

The group and I gradually entered a dead forest full of fallen, boney, and rigid branches. There was nothing around us but slim, lifeless trees appearing to be the very essence of the word soulless. I guessed to myself we wouldn't find any LifeTrees within it. It looked too . . . grim to possibly contain any. The forest was so extensive that when I looked to the left and right, I couldn't see the edges of it.

"How dense is this forest? How far will it go?" I wondered, shifting my eyes around.

I looked over my shoulder at Regor. His Treye was shining.

"Regor. Is something the matter?" I asked with caution, but with a bit more of an intruding tone. He didn't answer me right away. Instead, he closed his eyes and put his right hand on his Treye. His suit's indents, including the triangular indents on the palms, began to shine a brilliant lavender. I felt his energy flow through me as my suit softly vibrated in resonance.

Regor's suit and Treye progressively shimmered brighter and brighter for a minute until going back to their normal shades. He opened his eyes and looked over to me.

"Samuel, it would appear that I've neglected to inform you of my predominant ability. The level in which I sense energy can sometimes range for hundreds of meters. But only to those who are not masking their energy." He began squinting through closed eyes.

"So that's what you can do," I thought. He continued. "I have come to the conclusion that it is indeed other beings that I am sensing. Here in these woods. They are not like beings of the blank slate. And do not feel as if they've been touched by you, Samuel. . . . They've . . . been indoctrinated by Leumas. . . ." Gasps of nearby beings in the crowd behind us followed Regor's words.

Buster spoke. "So you're saying the enemy is close by!?" He reached for his weapon. But before he could take it off his back, Regor held up his hand in his direction to calm him.

I spoke up. "Can't we just go around them? This forest is huge."

Kobe's voice answered my question. "No. We need to go directly through the forest. The enemy is most likely expecting us to notice them and go around. They'll be prepared for it." I looked at him through the sides of my eyes.

"You know, for somebody who doesn't like talking much, he seems to be pretty chatty," I almost said aloud.

Leira spoke up in agreement after taking a step forward. "He's right. It'll catch them by surprise." Everyone looked around, searching for anyone to counter.

Regor broke the silence. "As of right now, I don't possess enough control over my ability to pinpoint their location. I know only that they happen to be in the direction we are currently headed."

Sandy jumped in the moment the last word left his lips. "Well, then I say we should waste no time! We were going to have to run into them eventually! I'm going in!" She reached into the pockets of her utility belt and grabbed a crystal blade with each hand. Her indents began to shine neon yellow to contrast the burgundy of her suit.

"Sandy, you mustn't be rash! We don't have enough information on the enemy or their abilities yet. We should plan before striking!" Regor exclaimed.

Sandy blew him off and kept on with her preparations. "I'm the *scout*. Remember?" she mocked.

Regor showed some irritation to the sass. I felt a smirk beginning to form before I choked it down as to not smile at an improper time.

She continued. "If I'm in any sort of trouble, I'll raise my energy until it's completely noticeable to you. Until then, it'll be concealed. Got it?" She didn't wait for a reply. She knelt down almost to the ground, slid her left leg back a couple of feet, and then took off faster than humanely possible, leaving behind afterimages on the sides of trees she used to push off of.

Just like that, Sandy was out of sight.

"Well, now we have no choice but to go straight ahead," Regor said after a quick sigh. He paused before continuing.

"The entire group must all travel within my sensory field. This way, I'll be able to know if and when any of us come in contact with an enemy being. Buster will undoubtedly have to go with Samuel to the point of contact. Buster will subdue the being, and Samuel will then attempt a **conversion**."

I shifted uncomfortably. "Will I even be able to . . . 'convert' them to a nature like yours? What does that even mean?"

Buster took a step forward. "There's only one way to find out," he said tersely.

Leira looked in my direction. "What do you think Samuel?" she asked.

I slicked my hair back. Despite how cold I knew it was, I felt beads of sweat forming on my forehead. The huge group behind us all looked to me as if I was capable of making a decision.

"It's worth a shot. If we can help these people without hurting them, all the better." Regor and I made eye contact.

"Onward then," he said without breaking it.

After the crowd behind us formed a circle around Regor to fit within his sensory range, we moved forward. I couldn't help but feel a bit anxious as we trudged through the dead forest. The crunching and snapping of brittle twigs, being the only sounds heard, vibrated through the air.

The smell in the air was woodsy, and the sky was grey and pale. I looked over my right shoulder at the crowd behind me. Most of the beings were looking straight ahead, but there were some darting glances in different directions nervously.

"Different personalities react differently," I thought. I turned my head back around before I let their fear affect—infect—me.

I let out a low sigh, but Leira still heard it. She looked at me until I looked back.

"What's on your mind, Sam?" she asked.

I waited a few seconds before replying back. "Yeah . . . I'm just a little on edge now that I know at any mo—" mid-sentence I started to feel an odd swirling in my stomach. The feeling had enough force to stop me from finishing my word, and even prevented me from moving. Regor walked around me and then turned to see why I had stopped. But before he had a chance to inquire further, his Treye glowed to its maximum brightness instantaneously. His eyes shot open as he looked around frantically. It was too late.

"NO!" he yelled. We all followed his scream to what he was looking at.

A cry for help caged within a gasp of pain and misery pierced the air. Just about ten meters away was one of the beings from the crowd. He had been impaled right through the center of his chest and was being held up in midair by the weapon; his trembling hands desperately gripping onto the perpetrator's blade, with blood sliding down his leg, eventually forming into individual drops hitting the ground with regretful abandon. Leira gasped in remorse. My eyes were peeled to the being. The being without mercy.

He was a male, with silver hair that was long enough to reach midway down his back. His eyes were cold and fierce, and he had chin hair forming a sharp point. His Treye that was supposed to be purple was a deep red and glowed brightly. He was dressed in what looked like armor with heavy black crystals growing out of the back of it like spikes. The gloves had sharp tips like the gauntlets of the Middle Ages and had a red glow to each fingertip. The weapon he used was a black crystal sitting on the top of his wrist and protruding out a little under a meter long.

I squinted, thinking that it had to be him. The one. The first being. But a headache came on swiftly before I could think more about it. Before another few moments, I was debilitated, just as I had been back in Crystal City. I dropped to my knees and the visions began again.

Again, I saw through the eyes of Leumas. I was midway through striking a being at the first village. The one he chose to be his first victim.

After a few moments, the struck being looked back scornfully; a perspective I hadn't seen while watching from afar.

And then suddenly my eyes were forced shut. Only to open inside of a pyramid. The same being, a little further into his evolution, stood before me (in the body of Leumas) like a subservient military private.

"I said . . . get it done!!" Leumas yelled. The roar of his voice, felt in my own throat.

Again, my eyes shut and re-opened to a new scene. An empty field with men in helmets watching on in the distance. The being, in front of Leumas again, had longer hair. He stood above a group of fallen beings as crystals encased him, creating crystal-like armor. A blade formed, extending from his forearm as if it grew naturally. The same blade impaling the being outside the vision.

Leumas walked over and put a hand also encased in crystal on his shoulder. He gripped it tightly and said, "Now go, Invidius. Find them."

I was thrust out of the vision. I breathed heavily and just barely held my head up to see what was in front of me.

Invidius retracted his arm back, splattering the leftover blood onto the ground of the forest; effectively removing the weapon so quickly the other being fell to the floor only after the crystal was completely pulled out of his body.

Buster rubbed his fingers together before gripping onto his weapon. I squinted at that with familiarity but was pulled from the thought as he took his weapon out from behind his back. It was the first time I had actually looked at it.

Besides the handle, the weapon was made entirely of the clear quartz-like crystal. It was a huge axe with the shape of the Merkaba above the head of it. The pole of the axe was a bit curved and also looked as though it was sharpened.

I was speechless. I couldn't tell Buster to hold off, and I didn't think I wanted to anyway. I found myself wishing Sandy hadn't run off. She was the only other true fighter in the group it seemed like. It was all up to Buster. If he couldn't stop Invidius, nobody could.

Suddenly the indents on Buster's suit began to shine a bright red. Buster also became more vascular, pumping blood through his muscles all over his body. The energy I felt coming from him was immense. I found it almost hard to breathe just being in his presence. He lowered his head for just a moment and then rushed at Invidius with full force and intensity. Invidius raised his hand casually with an arrogant smirk.

Just before Buster's axe would have come in contact with his skull, another being dressed similarly to Invidius jumped into the line of fire. The scapegoat being simply allowed himself to be slaughtered for Invidius to live.

As the sacrificed being lay lifeless on a coffin of twigs and dirt, all Invidius could do was snicker carelessly. It made me sick to my stomach. I felt my Treye burn up a bit. I wanted to do something but knew I couldn't.

I realized a moment or two later we were surrounded by a large group of Invidius's men. They all had helmets on that had a visor in the shape of an upside-down triangle, with the rest of the helmet having a sleek design. Their suits were skin-tight and black with small, slightly dull crystals growing off of their backs; all of them carried sharpened crystal spears. They were all uniform; the same as one another in appearance and goal.

The idea of giving up surged through the corners of logical thought within my brain. I balled up my fists, gripping them tighter and tighter as my thoughts progressed.

"We were never going to avoid the fight," I thought, deflated.

All of a sudden, I felt a hot wave of energy coming from our group. The people in the crowd were definitely frightened and inexperienced, but they were united. And they weren't about to just lie down and die. Confidence was instilled within me. I gritted my teeth and made eye contact with Invidius.

"You're . . . not going to get away with this. You goddamn monster," I said just above the volume of what would be considered under my breath.

As I finished my final word, beings within my group spread out and began to attack Invidius's men. Buster continued his assault on Invidius himself as Leira and Regor circled around me.

Regor spoke up. "We need to relocate. This isn't a satisfactory environment for the securing of your life, Samuel." Leira nodded. I was silently resistant to the idea, not wanting to be a coward. Regor immediately picked up on it.

"Listen, Samuel, this isn't the time for empathy or noble heroics. You must SURVIVE this battle." After pausing for a moment, I reluctantly agreed, allowing them to escort me deeper into the forest.

I turned around when we were far enough away from the chaos. At that point, we weren't even able to hear the clashing of crystals and the cries of pain. A sliver of regret bubbled up inside me.

"We have to go back for them!" I yelled to Regor. He replied to me with a calmer voice than mine.

"In time we will, Samuel. Timing is so very important. . . . Now that they are not repressing their energies, I will be able to easily identify the status of the enemies and the group. We will then assess when and how the proper approach should be carried ou—"

"We don't have time for that!" I yelled. But before I could continue to make my case, Regor's Treye shined on its own once again. He looked around in all directions before brandishing an involuntarily distraught expression.

"Sandy!"

CHAPTER 13

The Transformation

T he spots of blood on the nearby branches were still fresh and hadn't dried up just yet. The contrast of the red on the white branches looked beautifully horrid. A powerful breeze swept through the area.

We stood about a meter from what stole the breath from us. I felt a bit of rage build up within me. I looked down at Sandy. She laid there, possibly lifeless, with a wound starting from her hip, extending upward diagonally to her collarbone. Blood still leaked from her unconscious body onto the ground of the forest.

Regor looked at Leira, nearly hopeless. She nodded and got down on her knees, positioning her hand over Sandy's gash.

Her Treye glowed, and the indents on her suit shined a brilliant violet around her hands. I looked on, shocked to find out Leira's ability.

"Leira . . . you can—"

"Yes. Heal any wound. It's more of a reverse in time than actually healing." I squinted my eyes shut and turned around. Regor sensed my decision.

"You can't go!" he yelled in my direction.

"If we don't do something, they'll all end up like Sandy."

Regor paused for just a second before replying. "I cannot stop you from doing what you think is right. However, allow us to regroup and plan—" The word "plan" sparked my interruption as I realized . . .

"Where's Kobe?" I asked, looking around. Regor continued his speech, but it all disappeared into a murmur behind the curtain of my ringing ears. I couldn't get the thought of Kobe not being with us out of my mind. Something felt wrong about it.

"Are you even listening to me!?" Regor asked, cutting through my fog-lined perspective. I directed my attention back to him.

"Yes, Regor," I replied a little halfheartedly looking back at Leira. Regor grunted in response, not convinced.

I squatted down and looked at Sandy's face. There was blood in her red hair. The reds and oranges juxtaposed tragically and beautifully against her ivory skin. It was a grim painting of warm hues. Her wound was nearly sealed up.

Suddenly, Sandy's eyes blew open, giving everyone quite a shock. She struggled to get back up but failed.

"AARGHH! Dammit! I've got to get back and fight!"

"Sandy, just relax now. He's gone now. Buster's got him covered."

"Not without me he doesn't!" She tried to get up again, a bit more successful than last time, but she still fell. The wound opened back up a little. She grunted in pain. Leira sighed.

"Sit still, Sandy. . . . In fact, this might take a while." She darted a glance at me, then Regor, then back at me.

"You should go check on the others. We'll follow you shortly." I turned to Regor and awaited his response. Regor clutched his nasion.

"Fine. I see that there's just no way to convince you otherwise. But we do this **my** way. We go around and catch him by surprise. We might just have one chance at this."

We turned back toward the way from which we had come. Terrible energy emanated from that entire direction. I could just . . . feel it. Genocide. It was a genocide.

We hurried back, progressively picking up the pace while dodging hanging branches and snapping weak twigs. We were silent the entire way back. I ran as fast as I could for the last few moments, and Regor struggled to keep up.

We burst through the clearing. There were only about twenty beings from our group still left and easily double the number of Invidius's men. Dead bodies were scattered around the entire surrounding area, leaving blood spills and splatters everywhere I looked. The battleground reminded me of photographs from America's first Civil War. But pictures could never *really* give you the true impression of what living through it felt like. Even the wars on Earth I had witnessed were mostly fought at a distance. This was all right before my eyes. An absolute horror to witness.

Buster was in a blind rage. He was wildly swinging his axe, shouting with every attempted blow. There was an immense difference in speed between them. Buster had little to no chance of touching Invidius, let alone cutting him down.

Buster's indents blared red, and the suit was torn in a few places, exposing deep cuts that looked painful. Invidius toyed with him; evading every whirl of the axe as if Buster was a child wielding a wooden sword. Invidius smirked the entire time, thoroughly enjoying the clash. I tightened my fists. Regor spoke up quietly.

"We have to wait for the right moment." I gritted my teeth impatiently.

Just as I was going to give in and rush toward them, it happened. Invidius grew more impatient than I. He forced his sharpened crystal straight through Buster's chest as he had with the first being that had begun the fight. Buster stood there, motionless at first, before reaching for the blade with a shaking hand. Just then, Buster dropped his axe. I saw it fall to the ground as it symbolized the moment in which Buster had no more strength left to fight back. I couldn't see or focus on anything else. I stood there looking at the fallen weapon with tunnel vision that seemed to shake with the rest of my body. My mouth dropped as my eyes widened.

My breathing became heavier and heavier. Regor looked at me with worried eyes. My indents began to shine a clear transparent white that progressively turned solid and bright. The aura around me made the dirt at my feet move away from my body. I noticed my eyesight started to blur, and I was losing control of myself. I couldn't stop what was beginning.

My perceptive suit was transforming.

Crystals shot out from my back, with a considerably large one protruding from my wrist like Invidius's weapon. The organic suit was truly a marvel. For it to actually be alive enough for the crystals to literally grow off of my back in seconds amazed me. The power was intoxicating. I felt an overwhelming urge to take anything out in my path.

Suddenly, I noticed everybody on the battlefield looking at me. All of the fights around us had seized. While Invidius's men were distracted by my aura, the few still alive in our group walked over and joined me. It was quiet. All I could hear was the groaning of pain coming from Buster and a few others awaiting death. I looked around for a few seconds and then directed my attention to Invidius. We made strong eye contact, staring each other down for what felt like an eternity. He roared with laughter and then went back to being serious in an instant.

"I see you've achieved the crystalline form." He pulled his weapon out of Buster without even looking at him and started to walk toward me. My transformation made me appear similar to Invidius.

"Leumas prophesied this. He knew you'd eventually take the form. Robust emotional output is all it takes. Simple enough for a human. All you know is how to follow your deterministic, knee-jerk responses...." The look in his grey eyes was intimidating and dangerous. He smiled.

"Are you upset, Samuel? Are you mad that I played a little too rough with your friend here?" Invidius turned halfway to point my attention to Buster. He took a few steps back toward him and then squatted down beside his damaged body.

"A fool. But a good dog." He belittled Buster by petting his head.

"That's a little ironic. Coming from you," I replied with a blood curdling calm I forced upon myself. His smirk disappeared.

"Come then. You think your result will be any different?" Something snapped within me. I lost control over my body entirely. I immediately charged at him with blind intentions, but just before I reached him, my Treye purged out a massive amount of red, blinding light. I couldn't see or feel anything.

One moment I was in the forest, and the next moment I floated in the middle of a white abyss. I looked around in all directions but couldn't see anything tangible. After a few moments of perplexity, my entire body began to vibrate softly. A misty cloud of violet color materialized before me. The haze began to form into basic shapes that with time, formed details.

Eventually, the Eye itself from Crystal City appeared. It stared through my very soul, making me feel as though I had thousands of tiny pins throughout the inside of my body. I looked directly into the Eye, hoping to gain something from the experience.

My brain was absolutely assaulted with visions. First, I saw a distressed Ariel move further and further away, then a dimly lit table with a suitcase on it, the one when I had brokered . . . the deal . . . and then it all dissolved into a fiery mushroom cloud.

I started to feel drowsy. I thought falling asleep wouldn't be a great plan considering the situation, but I was completely delirious and had no idea why I wasn't controlling my body in the first place, let alone why I floated in some sort of twilight zone. And so I allowed myself to fall into a powerful, albeit *v*ery comfortable, slumber.

CHAPTER 14

The Betas

I felt like I had taken a quick power-nap on a crowded train. I went from me having no idea where I was or what I was doing to me striking Invidius instantaneously. His blade parried mine, deflecting my blow, sending me back a couple of steps. I wanted badly to know why the hell I was just somewhere else, but that was the least of my worries.

"Keep them busy," said Invidius to his men. The others in our group rejoined the fight as well.

While still in a daze, I attempted to slash at Invidius. He expertly parried my blows one after another. The sounds the crystals made while clanking into each other were unlike any sound I had heard while on Earth or the new planet alike. It was almost as if the sounds were delayed and then echoed after each consecutive counter.

My barrage of untrained and uncoordinated strikes proved to be a series of fruitless exchanges. I tried jumping up and landing down on top of him. I wanted to use gravity as a way to power my strike, but this ended up being a way to open me up to a swift block and then a kick to my chest, effectively knocking me off balance.

He then thrust toward me and forced his blade to my sternum. I stumbled to the ground. The tip of his weapon made contact with my armor and caused it to crack and tear a bit. He pushed harder, successfully getting through my suit and drawing blood. At this moment, I figured it was all over. My eyes looked back at him shakily. I was at his mercy. I lost the strength of my resolve within seconds.

Just then, Leira and Sandy got back to the scene. Leira glared toward Invidius, Treye shining at full intensity. And with uncanny timing, Invidius stopped. They shared a few moments of piercing eye contact.

Invidius retracted his blade and made a "humph" with a smirk.

"Leumas probably wants the pleasure of taking you down himself anyways. But this was fun." He looked at me as he stood up, plaguing me with discomfort.

Invidius's men killed off a few more beings, then followed Invidius, who had started walking away already.

I lay down completely and hit the ground with a weak hammer fist. Invidius spoke under his breath while disappearing deeper into the Dead Forest, smile still intact.

"Then again, if you die at the **Betas**' hands, it isn't on my head." I squinted, wondering what he could have meant by that. Regor helped me to my feet.

My suit vibrated as it retracted the crystals and patched up the hole caused by Invidius. I winced in pain as I rubbed my fingers over the area just covered. Leira, noticing Buster, rushed over to him.

"He's still alive. . . . But . . ." Regor said softly. I walked over slowly, looking down at Buster, guilt-ridden. Leira began healing him. I stared at her for a few moments.

"Leira . . . what did you say to Invidius? How did you make him stop . . . ?"

"I reminded him that if Leumas was so powerful, he'd want to kill you himself. . . . I said what I had to, . . ." she replied immediately, as if she knew I was going to ask. I watched her silently before peering over at Sandy. She appeared as though nothing had happened to her. Her suit mostly patched up the slice, and her attitude and folded arms let me know she was mentally back to normal as well.

I let out a sigh of relief, but then suddenly remembered all the others. I took a look out at the aftermath of the battle. A harrowing sight. Hundreds if not thousands, dead. Dead like ants after fumigation. The whole lot of them, minus a dozen or so still clinging to life, meditating. I didn't even know any of their names. My heart sank.

Buster gasped for air violently before coughing up blood. A collective "Buster!" was heard by Regor and Sandy. They did have time to learn his name. Get to know him. Care about him. His loss would have weighed much heavier on them then on me.

"I could only imagine how they could be feeling about the entire city being slaughtered . . ." I thought somberly. Buster spoke up through grumbled speech.

"I couldn't even land one hit on that silver-haired prick!" Just before Leira could tell him to calm down, Regor turned his head quickly behind him, gritting his teeth. After a moment, we heard leaves crunching in the distance.

"Samuel, it would be wise to reform that armor. Whoever is coming is masking their energy," Regor said, without looking away from the mystery of the forest. I nodded.

After a few attempts of squeezing my muscles, grunting, and standing with a tight foundation . . . nothing.

"I-I don't know how to do it. I don't think I can." As I finished my sentence, a figure poked its head out from the thick of the forest. It was Kobe. Everyone lowered their shoulders at once.

"Kobe, where you been, man??" Sandy asked with not so hidden snark. Kobe walked over to us slowly.

"My abilities are not fit for physical confrontation. And since I'm a vital part of this group, I secured my safety." His words were met with unease and mild disdain from everyone in the group. Sandy rolled her eyes and turned her back to him.

"The nerve on this guy," I thought with a raised eyebrow.

I looked at Leira She seemed focused on healing; Buster was close to stabilizing.

"Hey, Leira. When you're finished up with Buster, there are plenty of others in the group that need help," I said. Leira responded promptly.

"I have but two hands, Samuel. I'll do all that my body permits of me. They'll get healed." My stomach turned a bit anxiously. She noticed.

"You should relax. It's getting late. It'll be dark soon. . . . Let's build a fire." She looked at Regor, and then back at me. "Regor, why don't you two go collect some wood while I'm finishing up here?" Leira took notice of me staring down Kobe.

"Don't worry. Since he didn't *do much* in the last hour, I'll put him to work with me, gathering some wood as well." I continued darting Kobe with a speculative glance before feeling a hand on my shoulder. It was Regor.

"Go with her, Kobe. She'll need the extra pair of hands after she's done with Buster. We should let the other two get some rest," said Regor. I decided to drop my suspicions for the moment. I had a job to do now. Regor spoke again.

"Let's head out. Should be easy enough to find wood in this dead forest." I smirked for half a second, recalling a small wave of nostalgia.

"We've got to make sure to find thicker logs. Ones that won't just burn up quickly though, Regor."

"I'm aware," he replied dryly. My smirk returned for an encore. That is, until I remembered how the day had been going once again. The smirk erased itself, leaving a melancholic frown behind.

We had ventured out further than I thought we'd need to. The deeper we went into the forest, the less I thought about how far out we had gone and the more I wanted to reminisce about the memories of Earth before the war. I decided to make some small talk with Regor.

"So . . . Regor . . . tell me a little more about yourself." He didn't look up at me. He kept on searching the area for the right branches like a biologist looking for a female endangered animal. He replied while still looking down.

"I haven't any more to tell you about myself. My entire consciousness formed all but a few days ago." I awkwardly awaited a clever response to find its way into my head. I changed the subject instead.

"Right. Yeah. Um . . . ok . . . so what do you think about Invidius?" The temperature dropped, allowing our suits to accommodate with thicker texture on command once again. I looked back from where we had come from. Regor responded.

"They don't bode well for our chances against Leumas. . . . We're just going to have to hope you can talk him out of this. Or convert him. . . . It's best to just forget about them for no—" but before he could finish, he darted a glance outward in absolute distress, Treye shining brightly.

Just then, he shoved me with all his might before leaning back swiftly. A long, thin, and extremely sharp crystal whizzed right in between us, plowing through a tree's bark like it was made of paper. Shards of wood cascaded through the air chaotically. The bark behind us had a huge hole in the center of it, causing the tree to begin falling in our direction.

"Watch out!" I yelled while leaping out of the way. I got up and frantically looked to see if Regor had dodged it.

"Regor?! You alright?"

"Yes! I'm fine! You?!"

"Yeah . . . barely. What the hell was tha—" My question was silenced by thunderous stomps booming in the distance. They moved closer and closer, quickly becoming more threatening and earth shattering.

Suddenly, just as it got within a dozen meters or so, it stopped. Regor and I were glued to the large, shadowed form hidden behind the thickness of the forest. A bright-red light pierced the darkness. It was an enormous red Treye. The owner of the massive triangular mark took a few more steps into a clearing, revealing itself.

"Regor . . . is that what I think that is?"

Before us stood a terrifyingly and immensely large Tyrannosaurus Rex.

"What . . . What the hell is a T. Rex doing here?"

On its back, looked like one of Leumas's men. He sat on a thin saddle with his legs secured to crystal casings. He had a single crystal spike jetting out of his helmet, and he had a bow with crystal arrows as his weapon. His Treye shined brightly, followed by his beast's.

The T. Rex let out a **monstrous** roar. The power of the sound was enough to knock weaker branches off of tress and shake the very ground beneath us. I was absolutely petrified.

Leumas's soldier reached for an arrow in his quiver. Regor grabbed me by the arm and started running with me.

"Come on, Sam!" he yelled, breaking my fear-stricken stance.

We ran as fast as we could, trying our hardest to dodge low branches and to not trip over fallen twigs. Adrenaline blasted through my veins, causing my suit's indents to light up. Vibrations around my legs shook violently as the suit tried to help reduce fatigue and give my muscles more control over quick movements.

I looked back, noticing the soldier pulling back his arm. Energy swelled around his hand, possibly enhancing the arrow's strength and potential energy. The arrow quickly followed.

I threw myself onto the ground, barely dodging the attack. The arrow ripped through another tree like it was casually bursting a bubble. The T. Rex roared once more and then began charging at us.

The ground shock, causing the smaller twigs to hop up around us as we continued to flee desperately.

I funneled every thought I had into telling my perceptive suit to make me faster and faster. It tightened and thickened until I ran at a superhuman speed, leaving Regor behind me.

"How fast am I running?! I can't even hear the stomps anymore," I thought before deciding to look back. My eyes shot open as I realized the T. Rex had just stopped. They had caught up to Regor, and the beast was staring him down. They were about to go for the kill.

"No!" I said under my breath before bolting over.

The T. Rex went in for a chomp. The teeth slapping together was an unsettling reminder of the monster's bite force. Regor just barely slipped between its legs. He kept circling around them, moving in and out of its field of vision. The rider grew tired of the chase quickly and went for another arrow. This time he didn't take the extra time to strengthen it. He went for speed.

"Regor, watch out!" I yelled in vain. The arrow, lightning fast, pierced right through Regor's thigh like a hot knife through butter. He crashed into a pile of dead branches and leaves yelling out in pain.

The rider reached behind him to ready another arrow. I watched on fearfully, not knowing what to do. My vision began to blur for a few moments. Suddenly, my suit began to vibrate wildly. I was transforming once again. This time, the crystals growing out of me were thinner and icicle-like. Instead of a blade protruding from my forearm, a bow made of crystal formed, attached to my back. I immediately understood.

I didn't hesitate to break the bow off; and with one of the crystals on my back as an arrow, I aimed for the rider. The indents on my suit lit up around my hands.

"*I can't miss. I **won't** miss*," I thought powerfully, with intention.

I squinted and let go of the crystal arrow. Just before the rider let go of his own arrow, mine knocked the bow right out of his hands. The hit caused him to lose balance and slip off of the T. Rex. As he fell to the ground, the color of the Treye in the center of the T. Rex's forehead changed from red to white.

After a moment or two, the T. Rex directed its attention to the rider. The being grunted in peril as he tried to run away.

The T. Rex followed, and in no time caught him. He chomped him once to stop him from moving, and then proceeded to finish him off with a few more.

I returned my attention to Regor and ran over to him. I took a look at his leg. There was blood everywhere.

"Shit, Regor . . . can you stan—"

"Yes, I can stand, Samuel. Now help me up." I hoisted him up. He winced in pain. Blood leaked through the gigantic hole in his thigh. Regor's suit reacted, tightening and thickening around the wound, successfully sealing it up.

"How come your suit stopped the bleeding but Sandy's and Buster's didn't?"

"It's because I'm conscious enough to tell it to. Barely. They weren't." He winced in pain again.

I looked over my shoulder. The T. Rex was in the distance, finishing up its meal. Regor spoke up.

"I noticed that the legs' holsters served as a way for the rider to maintain a direct connection to it. Without the crystal's enhancements, the beast can do whatever it pleases. In this case, eat its maste—"

"Regor. More walking, less talking." He nodded without a word as I helped him limp away. We were silent until we disappeared even deeper into the forest.

CHAPTER 15

The Stump

Before we knew it, a thick blanket of night covered everything in sight. It was dark enough to render our vision nearly useless. Since we weren't near any towns with crystals or any purposely grown LifeTrees, the only visible light was the occasional shine from Regor's Treye, and the faint glow of the moon phasing through the thick clouds. We pressed on without any thought to what direction we were actually going in. I wondered if we would eventually make it back to the group. I bit the corner of my lip and slicked my hair back.

"Anything?"

"No. Impossible to tell where they are. This forest is enormous," Regor responded.

"Oh . . . well how you feeling?"

"I'll be a bit better after this," Regor said while pulling a LifeFruit out from one of his pockets. My eyes widened. I dismissed my hunger though, knowing he needed it far more than I did. He ate it all in one bite, moments later not even needing me to help him walk anymore.

"So, uh, any idea where we're going, Regor?"

"No clue. And it's pitch black now. We'll never find them if we can't see or sense them. They could be masking their energies out of fear of the enemy. We should set up camp in the next clearing." I nodded.

The crinkling of dried, dead leaves beneath our feet rang through my ears as if they were inches from my eardrums. I stopped for a moment and picked one of them up. It was delicate enough to crumble almost instantly.

"One day, after all this is over, we gotta come back and plant some LifeTrees here. The place needs it," I said softly.

I let the crumbs from the leaf fall naturally from my palm before noticing something in the distance. I squinted my eyes to make sure I wasn't just imagining it.

"Regor, you see that? That blue glow?" Regor squinted too and nodded. The glow disappeared softly and slowly. I titled my head in curiosity. Regor darted a glance my way before following me as I continued toward it.

It shined once again for two seconds, stopped, and after a few seconds, repeated the process. A thin fog began to surround us.

The closer we got to the light, the thicker the fog got in turn. The ground beneath us changed from the dry and rigid surface we had been used to to a smooth and damp one that had a bit of a squish to every step. The light appeared concentrated in one area. I inched closer in wonder.

In the center of a clearing there was a tree stump with a group of mushrooms growing out of it, one much taller than the rest. The roots and the surrounding area on the ground, was lit a dim fluorescent orange. On top of each mushroom, was an outline of the Merkaba glowing a bright, neon blue.

I focused on the tallest one, mesmerized by its radiant color and the light it emitted. I began to reach out almost outside of my own control. In my peripheral, I noticed Regor looking at me with a "you shouldn't touch it" face. I decided to ignore his warning and put my hand just above the tallest mushroom. Condensation had formed on its head. I couldn't tell if it would be slimy or just wet to the touch. But I didn't care.

Regor snapped his attention to the surroundings. His Treye's light, cut through the momentary darkness.

"Something . . . is here. All around us. I couldn't feel them at first. But now—" A blurry image zipped past us in the distance where the tree-line began again on the other side.

A few more thumps and moist, squishy sounds echoed through the clearing. My heart started pounding as the mushroom grew dark once again. Regor widened his stance and began to breathe harder.

We both darted our heads around, impatiently waiting for the light to glow again. The glow appeared, revealing nothing. It went dark after the same two-second interval.

The light shined, as per the cycle. This time, it hypnotically drew me in. The color was truly fascinating. I was enraptured by its beauty like a mosquito on a lampshade. The outline of the Eye was brighter than the rest, creating soft beams of light through the fog surrounding us. I cautiously reached for the mushroom again. I couldn't help myself. I wanted to time my touch to the moment it lit up.

I reached for it, but before my fingers could actually graze it, Regor realized and tried to grab my forearm. He was too late.

The moment I pushed down on it, the entire group of fungi began to glow several times brighter than before, exposing all that was hiding within the forest around us.

There were approximately thirty massive elk circling the area. They had much thicker antlers and appeared stronger and taller than normal elk. They resembled the Irish elk from the Prehistoric times of Earth.

Regor and I stood there, frozen. Not quite terrified, but not at ease. The light hadn't stopped glowing since I had touched the mushroom. I dug my fingers in a bit more just in case.

Suddenly, the elk began to cry out until they were all howling up at the sky. The largest, and clearly the alpha of the Group, was dead ahead. It slowly approached me.

I retracted my fingertip for a second but realized the light dimmed the further I was from it, so I quickly planted my finger back on it, followed by my entire hand. When my palm touched the surface, a sound of pressurized steam pushed out of a narrow opening, making a wicked hiss.

The area got much brighter with the added amount of contact. The alpha elk, now only a few feet away, stared directly at me with its humongous, bulbous, black, spherical eyes. They were glossy enough to reflect the brilliant blue and orange glows in a near perfect, albeit perspective-skewed, reflection.

The elk's hot exhale fumed onto my cold cheeks. It had a white Treye on its forehead that began to shine. The rest of the elk paced over, tightening the circle.

"*Is it . . . trying to communicate with me?*" I wondered, strengthening my grip on the mushroom again. I looked down at the stump. I turned my head in realization.

"*This is the stump of . . . a LifeTree. But who or **what** would destroy one?*" I thought.

The surrounding elk all abruptly looked out into the forest at once. Regor and I followed suit while hearing some scurrying a bit in the distance. I mentally decided to cover us in darkness; felt like we needed to hide from whatever could be coming.

My fingers trembled as I took them off of the mushroom. The area regressed into darkness again. The very instant the tip of my nail no longer touched the mushroom head, a calm yet firm telepathic yelp rang through my brain. It was the leader elk.

"*R*un." My eyes widened as I noticed we, including the elks, were being surrounded. It was too late.

CHAPTER 16

The Hunt

I wasn't allowed the proper amount of time to react to the elk's warning. Instead, my full attention was captured by the newest issue of the night. Coming from in between the trees, were ten feathered Utahraptors with a single of Leumas's men on each one of them. Their feathers were similar to the area's terrain, as the T. Rex's skin had been. Their Treyes all glowed, and their menacing snarls and sharp exhales were intimidating.

I looked at the men riding on their backs. They sat on saddles as well, and the men had spears instead of bows. Their helmets had sharp edges on them that clearly resembled the feathers on the raptors' heads.

They slowly moved in as the elks slowly moved away in unison. The herd of elk roared, one by one in random order, as if it was their way of telling the enemies to back off. My vision darted back over to the leader elk with a distressed expression. I had to think quickly.

"If I just run, the raptors will catch the elk, instantly devouring them; and shortly after, they'll come for us. How can I direct their attention away from the herd, even for just a moment? Giving them a chance to defend themselves?" I questioned with intense care.

"One mistake and it's all over," I whispered to myself.

Regor heard the "stss" in "it's" while I spoke under my breath and looked over at me. I returned the glance. He pointed at the mushroom and made a throwing hand motion. I understood what he meant, but I had to move quickly.

I grabbed one of the smaller mushrooms growing out of the stump and ripped it off; expelling a gooey discharge that wrapped its sticky sap all over my suit's glove. I tossed the mushroom up in the air and toward the right. The raptors couldn't help but glance over in the direction the still dimly glowing fungi was flying in. I used this very moment to first look at the leader elk; signaling to him it was time.

"Now!" I yelled telepathically. The leader elk used the distraction as a way to attack them when they were off guard. Regor and I both knew that was our chance.

We took off into the forest with some of the herd following behind us. Just a few seconds later, I picked up on a few cries of pain coming from some of the unlucky elk caught by the predators. I knew some of them would be killed; it was inevitable. But I wanted to find a way to help at least some of them.

"Maybe if I spread them out, I can take them on individually," I thought. It sounded like a good idea, until another thought popped into my head.

"I can't just take the being off of the raptor like I did with the T. Rex. They'll probably still attack the elks out of pure predatory instincts. I'll have to actually take them down too."

I gripped my fists tightly and began to concentrate on transforming into the crystalline suit once again. We ran faster and faster into the woods while periodically looking back at the herd. The first few elk were taken down, but it appeared like the raptors were commanded to continue onward toward Regor and me; and they were gaining on us.

I concentrated harder, but I just couldn't find my way into the well of power while running at full speed. I needed to stop and thoroughly calm my mind. But I knew if I stopped, they'd rapidly catch up and proceed to take bites out of me that not even the suit could help recover from.

"Still . . . regardless of the danger, even in the state I'm in now, without the crystalline suit . . . I'll do what I can!" I shouted in my head.

I stopped running and turned around. Regor noticed I stopped and clumsily halted as well.

"What the hell are you thinking?! There's too many of them!" His words flew in one ear and glided right out the other. I tried concentrating harder but was too distracted by the chaos.

A raptor caught up to us in no time. It shrieked as it dashed toward me. I watched on helplessly before an elk leaped in the way, bashing it and its rider with its mighty antlers.

The pair went flying into the woods, scattering twigs and dirt in every direction. The soldier lay on the forest floor, Treye no longer illuminated, unconscious. An idea wormed its way into my head. I switched my attention to the dinosaur as it struggled to get back up. Without a second to think, I ran toward it at full speed. It noticed me getting close and shot a lightning-fast attempt to chomp a piece of my arm. I dodged it, and then jumped with all my might onto its back. I commanded the perceptive suit to strengthen around my hands, and I gripped tightly to the creature's neck, holding on for dear life. It screeched out in resistance, throwing its head around violently. It didn't want a master. It *never* did. But after fumbling my legs around long enough, I found the holsters for the feet on the saddle. I shoved my feet in, desperately trying to hold onto the wild creature.

The second his toes hit the bottom of the crystal casings, my mind and its mind were completely linked. I felt an immense wave of pain and suffering. Enslavement, aggression, and killer instinct. It was infectious, and I had to fight to maintain my sanity and remember what I was actually trying to do. I controlled my breathing, and shortly after, its fidgeting came to a halt. With the newfound control, my suit went back to its original state. I noticed the screams of wounded and dying elk again. They were being picked off, one by one.

Just then, underneath all of the painful squeals, I heard a few faint human-like grunts. I saw Regor with his back flat on the ground, struggling under a raptor's talons pressing hard against his legs; almost as though it was attacking there deliberately. Regor yelped in pain. I looked around, not quite knowing how to control my reluctant steed.

"GO!" I yelled mentally. Without hesitation, it launched forward and bit the lackey off of the other raptor's shoulder, shaking its head while its teeth were sunken in.

Once the rider was on the ground and incapacitated, the other beast intentionally left Regor to finish off the solider with a couple more bites. I gulped at the site of it, silently hoping I wouldn't share the same fate. I turned to Regor, who struggled to get up.

"Get on quick! And grab his weapon!" Regor, forgetting about the pain, had his suit tighten around his legs for the hundredth time. He bravely jumped onto the riderless raptor and held tight like I had.

Suddenly, I heard another squeal and looked to my right. It

was another one finishing off a half-dead elk. I had mine tackle it with just enough force to successfully knock that soldier off of its back. Regor's new steed ran over to finish the solo raptor off with a swift bite to the neck.

Regor looked over at me and nodded. Our creatures let out a quick war cry as they took off toward the battling elk.

We rode back through the forest until another rider intercepted our approach. We swiftly ran over and bashed them right into a frail tree, shattering its fragile bark upon contact.

Regor moved in, thrusting his spear into the beast's thigh. As it fell to the ground, mine leaped in and finished it off with its sharp talons.

I looked out into the near-black abyss. A set of glowing Treyes paced their way towards us like a pack of predators trying to their catch prey off guard.

Everything was quiet for a moment.

Seconds later, the remaining raptor Treyes all rushed toward us at once.

"They must have communicated!" Regor yelled.

They quickly surrounded us, snarling aggressively. I desperately tried to use the crystalline suit's power once more. But just as I began to concentrate, they all leaped out at once.

They began scratching and biting us from all angles, ripping our raptors to shreds while we barely fended off the spear attacks from the soldiers.

Through it all, a rider managed to shove his spear right into my shoulder.

Another blade headed for my throat when a powerful, collective groan echoed through the forest. The remaining, alive elk gathered around us, in turn surrounding the pack of raptors.

The enemies formed a reverse circle, sending out a few growls at the elk.

Mine and Regor's steeds collapsed, sending us to the ground along with them. I commanded my suit to patch up my shoulder wound while wincing in pain.

One raptor decided to be daring and foolhardy, jumping into the air with the intention of landing on one of the elk. Instead, the alpha elk rushed under it, forcing it to land perfectly on its antlers. It roared ferociously, and with great vigor, smashed the helpless beast onto the ground, killing it and its rider instantly.

The others were quiet and looked a bit discouraged; especially considering there were only a few of them left. There was a pause of any movement while the soldiers contemplated their next move.

The raptors ran one by one through a gap in the circle of elk, successfully fleeing the scene without a fight; clearly outgunned.

I marveled at the awesome presence of the alpha elk. It bowed its head in thanks.

Its Treye began to shine as it stared through my soul. I felt compelled to, and so I walked over and touched its Treye, hearing its gruff, wise voice telepathically.

"Latent scars are the maps of self.
The cartographer always, self.
Recompense, when retreaded in our solace
lined abyss, only serves to echo
the musings of our suffering.
Actualization, is born out of meaning.
Born out of acceptance."

I took a few moments to analyze the elk's riddled speech while taking a step backward. The alpha elk shined its Treye, and two elk came forward to his left and right side. Both had minor wounds but looked strong and resilient.

Regor and I looked at each other and nodded.

"Thank you," I said simply but genuinely.

Without another word, the wise elk began walking away with the rest of the herd, disappearing into the thick of the forest.

The two steeds waited until the rest of them were gone, and then approached us slowly. I looked through the trees. The fighting had brought us to the edge of the forest with a savanna on the other side.

Regor noticed me and responded. "It would be in our best interest to retire here for the evening. We haven't found the others yet, and the sun will be rising soon."

I sighed. "You're right."

We settled down on some twigs and leaves, sat in a meditative position, and tried to doze off.

After a few moments, with closed eyes, I spoke up.

"I know you've seen my memories. You've seen my world. You've seen it waste away through my eyes. I've told myself I . . . That it wasn't me. . . . That it's more complicated than that. And I still don't know if I even believe that. But I can't help but feel like there was always more I could have done. And I *know* there were things I shouldn't . . . have done. Maybe if I had just . . ." I could somehow tell Regor looked at me with a single eye open, listening intently. I continued.

"I just want to do right by this world at least. . . . I'll try my damndest." A moment of silence between us caused a bit of sorrow to leak into my heart. I felt alone. Regor's voice prevented me from falling deeper into that pit.

"I have. I have seen it all. As did every single one of those people from Crystal City. As did Leira, Buster, Sandy, and

Kobe. We've all seen it. Seen you. And yet, here we are; following you."

"But that's what I'm—"

"I know, Sam. I know. But I, or anyone here, can only attempt to judge you on what your actions have been since you chose to help us." He paused before continuing.

"I'd say the man in front of me, really *is* trying to do right by this world. That's what matters to me. And what matters to all of us." I nodded silently as a single tear slid down my cheek.

I allowed the emotions to flow silently as I drifted into sleep.

Journal Entry #1000

One thousand entries. One thousand thoughts. Feels like it's been forever. And I guess in some ways it really has. Forever as a measurement of time is so subjective. So many things tend to be. I realize that more and more every day. Things are supposed to be getting better. And yet, some people are so damn resistant. Resistant to change; to help. It's almost like I have to force it on them. This technology can change their lives. Their city, their country! And yet here I am musing about it like a crazy person, talking to myself. I've been talking to myself for one thousand weeks. Maybe I *am* a crazy person. The fact that Ariel still haunts my dreams, all these years later, speaks to that. Ghost children, no ghost children. I can't escape it. I'm so tired of this. We need more money. More funding. I know of **one** way to get it. Not everybody wants Roger Kaine innovations tech. But I know of some who are dying to get their hands on the secret to its design. And yet if they do get access to it, what will they do with it? I honestly don't even want to think about it. Especially considering I'm all out of options.

THE FEARLESS EYE

CHAPTER 17

The Covenant

With a shocking jerk of my chest, I was jolted awake. I quickly inhaled, as if I had been holding my breath. I looked around. There were LifeTrees everywhere; all of them dimly glowing. The dulled reflection shined off of the material of my suit, which was encased within its crystalline transformation.

"How did I get here?" I wondered.

I smiled out of relief. I had been hungry for a while and wanted to get my fill. Without even thinking, I rose to my feet and walked over to the tree directly in front of me. My hands shook as I reached out to pluck a fruit. I widened my eyes and began to breathe heavily again. I felt like I was about to drink water after a long drought. The vibrant colors of the leaves and bark sparkled with beauty. I felt an overwhelming sensation that could only be described as bliss.

The moment in which I plucked a fruit, I heard the faint hum that came with it. It vibrated through me as it had before; except this time, it didn't stop; a deafening dance of delight. That is, until it progressively got louder; until it was all I could hear. Within seconds, every single tree around me began to burn. The humming became unbearable. I grunted out in pain and couldn't even hear my own voice.

Suddenly, I found myself going from standing among the LifeTrees to sitting upright on the cold ground. It was just a dream. An intense, realistic, and frightening dream. I inhaled slowly and exhaled even more slowly.

I slicked my hair back and then looked around me. The daylight illuminating my surroundings was a sight for sore eyes after the night Regor and I had been through. I took a few moments to play back the events from the night before.

"Jeez what a night ... It's amazing we even survived that," I thought.

I looked around for Regor. He was already up, standing with his back facing me. His right hand was on a tree's bark, and he was looking out through the edge of the forest at the savanna. The two elk stood still, facing the same direction as Regor. I got up and approached them.

"Finally up, huh? Good morning," he said without turning back to look at me.

"Heh heh yeah. Morning," I said, pausing before continuing.

"It seems to be a clear day out. I'm sure we'll find the others today without problem," I said with mild confidence.

He replied quickly. "I'm sure they'll use common sense. They'll try to meet us at the next village."

I felt skeptical about his assumption, but searching through the forest, and possibly getting lost again, didn't sound like the best idea either.

I turned to the elk, looked at them, and then glanced back at Regor.

The elks bent down in such a way that would allow Regor and me to climb on top of them. But before I could move toward one of them, Regor spoke up.

"You take the male. You're more of a fighter than I am. I'll take the female."

I couldn't resist chuckling. He replied to my laughter with a halfway agitated tone. "That's humorous, is it? I assure you, the female is far faster than the bulky male!" he proclaimed with a little bit of pride and a smidgen of humor.

I awkwardly mounted the elk. There weren't any saddles or connection crystals, but somehow, I could feel the elk would listen to me. Sitting high up on a sturdy elk boosted my confidence.

"Let us go!" I said with zeal.

We exited the forest for the first time in what felt like weeks. The flatland in front of us had three-meter tall trees with dry, dark-green leaves dispursed around randomly for miles. The ground had brown shrubs half a meter tall, covering about 90 percent of what was in sight. The sun was brighter and bolder than it had been since I first arrived. The elk underneath us began moving forward, leaving the forest behind without a thought to look back.

After an hour or two of riding through the savanna, I started to become consciously aware of how hungry and thirsty I was. It had been more than an entire day since I had eaten, and we had been through several different battles on top of that. I felt as weak as the trees from the forest. Regor spoke up before I had the chance to.

"You must be hungry. No, I didn't take another LifeFruit with me. I only had the one. Let's keep our eyes open for any.' It was more than hunger. It was exhaustion. It was the craving for the satisfaction of being satiated. I needed it.

"You don't have to tell me twice," I said. He didn't respond.

I went back to looking straight ahead. Just then, I noticed something shining far out ahead of us. It had to be a LifeTree. Without hesitation, I yelled, "Let's go!" and thoughtfully visualized moving toward it. The elk responded correctly to my command and took off immediately.

The sound of Regor shouting, "No! Wait!" faded as the distance between us grew. I had tunnel vision, looking directly at my target without wavering at all.

Before I knew it, I was within fifty meters of the LifeTree. My mouth salivated, and I could feel my body warming itself up in preparation for the intensity of the fruit entering my stomach. Yet just as I got close enough to actually reach out and grab it, I realized it was merely a small, perfectly shaped, crystal cube. It had been projecting the image.

"What the?—" I heard a faint yell. It was Regor.

I turned my elk around so that I could see him. I tried to make out what he was saying. It sounded like, "Nook dove you," but I knew that didn't make sense. I tried to listen harder as he got closer.

"Look above you!" he screamed.

I swiftly looked up, only to see a pterodactyl's talons swooping down next to me. Luckily, I was still on my elk as it scurried a couple of meters away just in time. The pterodactyl's talons grazed the ground, causing some dirt and shrubbery to be shredded to pieces. On top of the creature was once again an enemy soldier; had on flight goggles that looked remarkably similar to ones from the early twentieth century, exposing his chubby face and extremely dark-brown skin.

"Damn it!" he shouted out loud as the talons missed their mark. He had what sounded like a thick, Australian accent.

"Hey listen, mate. You're Samuel, right? I just want to—" He went on to say something, but I couldn't hear the entire sentence due to the gusts of wind coming from the flapping wings. My elk and I backed up a bit. I squinted at them defensively.

"These guys never quit," I thought to myself. I was getting fed up with these damn soldiers and their dinosaurs. I wanted to end this fight quickly.

While reminiscing about my impulsive decision to jump onto the raptor's back, I promptly decided to relive that moment. I hopped off of the elk and ran up to the pterodactyl as it was taking off again. Right before it was entirely out of reach, I jumped up and grabbed onto the base of its talons. It howled in anger and tried to shake me off by soaring through the savanna sky. I forced myself not to look down. Instead, I pulled myself up using the fact I was deceived by their cube to fuel my strength for vengeance. I grabbed onto one of its wings and peeked up at the man.

"There's no waaaay you got up here," he proclaimed in denial. I growled while using the remains of my strength to tackle him off of the flying creature, causing the both of us to swiftly fall toward the solid ground below.

*"Shit! I'm going to break my legs if I land on them. I might just break **anything** I land on. . . . I need support!"* I thought in peril.

Seconds before hitting the ground, the Perceptive Suit vibrated and expanded; creating a layer of something gooey in between the fibers of the suit all around my body. Upon impact, my fall was broken; successfully spewing what felt like a mass of extremely thick indigo sap from the LifeTree. It was genius.

The soldier yelped in pain. He hadn't any protection, and he landed on his side. He was covered in the sap. Some of my protective goo somehow helped him not completely shatter his ribs and hip, but he was still a little too hurt to move around.

After removing his flight goggles, I noticed his light-brown eyes had tears of anguish in them. He had large ears and a large nose as well. A few freckles and moles were scattered around his middle-aged face, leaving me surprised by his complex features. His hair was woolly textured, seemingly not well taken care of, and five or six inches in length. Just before I was able to say or do anything to him, the pterodactyl came swooping back down to take us out; yet moments before impact, the soldier yelled out to it.

"**Stop!**"

It instantly pulled back its talons and let out a roar, soon landing a few meters away.

"*Why is this one obedient? And if it does listen to his commands, why did the soldier tell it to stop in the first place?*" I asked myself. Regor and his elk arrived at the scene.

"What's going on?!' he frantically questioned. I ignored him and spoke directly to the soldier.

"Start talking. How did you know who I am? And where we were? Do you know where the others are?" The soldier took a moment to look at both Regor and me, then smiled.

"You not gonna ask me my name first?" he asked sarcastically just before chuckling. His snickering led to a wince in pain. I angrily grabbed his suit. The pterodactyl screeched out in defense, but the soldier put his hand out to calm it down again. He continued.

"Whether or not you ask it, I'll tell it to you. It's Willie . . ." he grimaced in pain and struggled to continue, "and believe it or not . . . I'm not your enem—" he passed out mid-sentence. I looked up at Regor, who had been standing right next to where I knelt.

"What do you think?" I asked. He shook his head, tightening and narrowing his lips in consideration. He answered pensively.

"I say you were on the right track. He knows something. And we need to draw it out of him."

Hours flew by, and the sun began to go down. Regor had gone out to look for firewood, and Willie was still asleep, snoring loudly and most likely dreaming of a better life. He lay there, flat on his back, sleeping like a child after drinking milk. He carelessly slept in front of his enemy without a single concern for his life. At this point, I was sure he was actually just sleeping and no longer completely passed out. I considered forcing him awake several times, but ultimately came to the decision not to go through with it.

I looked up at the pterodactyl. Its eyes hadn't left him since the moment he fell asleep. *"Does it actually care for him?"* I wondered.

"All of them thus far seemed to be cold-blooded killers. . . . But maybe this is all a facade. I don't know what to think anymore." That last thought alone, sent chills dancing through my spine. That level of wickedness would be something I had yet to experience in my entire life. I seriously hoped for the former.

While still lost in thought, Regor came back from his search for fallen branches. Without looking, I heard a fair amount of sticks and branches hit the ground, flattening the shrubbery, followed by Regor hopping off of his elk. It was time to make a fire.

The burning flames seemed to serve no purpose other than to calm our nerves. Our suits kept us warm, and we had nothing to cook. It reminded me of the day I first arrived on the planet. *"I'm just as hungry and lost now as I was back then,"* I thought. I chuckled and threw a twig I had been holding into the calm fire.

As if Regor could sense my thoughts, he spoke in accuracy.

"There's something *'human'* about making a fire. Something soothing. We don't need it considering our suits, and yet here we are, sitting around it willingly." I looked at him through new eyes. It was almost as if I was looking at just another human being I would have met on Earth.

"He's almost indistinguishable from one at this point."

I remembered the old camping trips I used to take again. The pleasant memories comforted me. The sense of camaraderie present on camping trips only served to strengthen my desire to reunite with the group. I was worried about Leira more than anything. I hoped Sandy and Buster had successfully fended off any threats that came their way. I hoped the raptors hadn't gotten to them. And I *really* hoped that if there was another T. Rex, it hadn't found them either. I sighed a long sigh and slicked my hair back.

I squinted and looked into the fire. The soft, orange glow being projected onto the uneven savanna ground was relaxing to watch. We were silent, daydreaming as we watched the embers fly around, listening to the crackles and pops that came on occasion.

The silence was soon broken by the pterodactyl spreading its wings and hollering. I looked over at Willie. He was yawning with his arms stretched out wide. He was finally awake.

Feeling like I didn't have a second to spare, I scurried over to him. The thoughts of potential betrayal had been quietly echoing within me since the moment I thought of them. After getting within a meter away, I cautiously drew closer, until he was within my reach. Just before he finished yawning, I grabbed him once again. He looked a bit startled as I clenched hard on his suit.

"A man can't even finish a yawn without you nearly strikin' him, can he?" he said sarcastically while grinning. It upset me.

"You listen to me. And listen to me good," I said, pointing my finger at him. The pterodactyl shrieked out in his defense. Mine and Regor's elk growled back at it. Willie answered me after calming the pterodactyl down again.

"You're an awfully grumpy man, aren't you? You haven't eaten in a while. That's it." I inhaled strongly and then squeezed tighter on his suit.

"I'm running out of patience. You need to answer my questions. **Now!**" I yelled out to him. It wasn't like me to get as irritable as I was. He might have been right. Between not having any food and not knowing whether or not the group was ok, I just wasn't in the mood for his folly.

Willie reached for his pouch and quickly pulled out a LifeFruit. He tossed it to Regor and then handed the pouch to me.

"Go ahead, mate. There's some more in there. And throw one to Wendell so he knows you don't mean to harm him, will you?" I didn't know what to say. I was so hungry, but I couldn't let it break my focus on getting answers. I was about to continue questioning when Willie noticed, cutting me off.

"Do you remember my name?" he asked me as if it held great importance. His wrinkled face displayed a serious expression for once.

"Why does that even matter?!"

He immediately replied, expecting that response. "Ah, but ma name isn't as superfluous as one would think. It's the fact that I even have a name, why it serves as an important factor." He smiled again. I was taken aback by his statement.

"So spit it out then. Why is it important . . . *Willie?*" I emphasized his name to give him humane value. For the first time since we began conversing, he broke eye contact. He looked a bit troubled while preparing his answer this time. His tone carried a longing sense of somber.

"Well. Not all of us can think on our own, ya know. Those 'created' as Betas are nearly mindless altogether. Betas are just soldiers. No thoughts to be had. I was meant to be an Alpha; like Invidius. It's why I have a name. However, after my personality took shape, I took pity on poor Wendell over there. He wouldn't be tamed. Leumas was ready to put us both down for the count. So I jumped on his back and we ran." I looked into his hazy brown eyes, puzzled.

"... Where is he? Where is Leumas?" Regor asked, still chewing on his LifeFruit.

"Glacial City. In the mountain range by the glacier bed. Where the other Eye is. He wants to change how our entire species operates. Be like the ancestors. Like some godforsaken emperor. He knew you'd stand in his way too." I was about to speak up, but Willie spoke over me again.

"Samuel. I may have been awakened by Leumas. But I assure you, I am not your enemy. We're not all where we come from."

I slowly let go of his suit, looking to Regor. Wendell finally relaxed in the distance. I took a few moments to take it all in. I slicked my hair back.

"Alright," I began. "So I'm public enemy number one, huh?" Willie looked directly into my eyes as he responded.

"Would you like to know why?" I was listening intently. I felt tingles *t*hroughout my body in wake of the answer.

"It's   because   Leumas   is   afraid   of   you."

CHAPTER 18

The Adversity

After speaking with Willie for a bit longer, Regor found himself growing tired and decided to rest. I could tell he was still skeptical, but exhaustion had taken hold. A few minutes later, Willie, still recovering from his wounds, closed his heavy eyes mid-sentence as he had before. I was left as the only one awake.

I let out a sigh while looking at the two of them. There was no way in hell I could sleep; not with all this new information floating around my consciousness. I lay down straight on my back and looked up at the magnificent, star-filled sky. The train of thought running through my mind was hopping from track to track, derailing itself, and changing pace with no real destination. Most of what I believed about the enemy, and all of what I had gathered through assumption, was in shambles.

I looked down at him, sleeping peacefully. His ruby-red

Treye glowed dimly as he lay there, vulnerable and defenseless in the hands of what was meant to be his enemy. Before he passed out for the second time, he had told me Leumas created the Betas; those who transformed into creatures.

*"If even **they** could feel, like Wendell and the elk do, then it's safe to say that any of them have the potential to do the same; even the raptors and the average foot soldier,"* I thought. I was troubled by that thought. I found it hard to feel sympathetic toward the soldiers that just killed nearly the entire group of villagers I was with. And hell, they nearly killed me too.

I had asked Willie about the wise leader elk and why he had more cognitive ability than Wendell or the other dinosaurs. It was fascinating to me the beings that became the Irish elk were the group of beings from the very first village. All but the first two touched by Leumas. Those were Invidius and Willie. That thought still perplexed me.

"It's wild to think that those two could be born under nearly the same circumstances and yet differ so much in personality," I wondered. They had more power than the others because they were the first to be converted. In turn, they were the first to be experimented on. The elk ended up escaping, desiring lives of their own. From then on, Leumas made the dinosaurs unable to speak clearly and nearly mindless.

I then thought of Invidius. I shivered with just the idea of his existence. I grasped my now thick facial hair while sitting with my legs crossed.

I also thought of how much action I had been involved in. I had done things I never would have dreamed of doing.

"Clashing weapons with an alien warrior? Shooting a man off of a T. Rex? Jumping onto a raptor? Pulling myself up onto a pterodactyl and then tackling the guy riding on it? Who have I become in a matter of days? Who the hell are you anymore?" I questioned while looking down at my tremoring hands.

"Keep it together! Dammit, Sam!" I spoke out loud.

Willie rustled around a bit and turned over. I glanced in his direction. He slept peacefully, grunting in the midst of slumber. I closed my eyes and let out another sigh. It gave me an idea.

Because I couldn't actually sleep, I decided on meditation, a much deeper meditation than on the previous nights. I recreated what Leira had taught me back at Crystal City. I sat up straight, kept my eyes closed, and began letting my mind flow, blending smoothly with the universe itself. I lost consciousness, yet gained more of a conscious span within that same moment. I slowly lost my grasp on time, drifting into the void of all and one.

My eyes slowly opened, revealing Regor and Willie in front of me sleeping. I noticed my glasses, still on my face, were now blurring my vision. I quickly took them off and realized how much my sight had improved. I was beyond questioning changes happening to me. I looked at the frames for a while as a farewell to all the memories they had brought me just before setting them down one last time.

It was morning, and we needed to get moving again. I gradually rose up to standing with my back straight. I stretched with my arms out wide, squinting in flexible delight. I felt loose, yet tight in all of the right areas. My breathing was perfectly free of any congestion I might have had, and my head was clear. Before trying to wake the others up myself, I decided to do a little experiment.

I walked over to Wendell, who looked as though he had been awake the entire time. I got a cold stare dead in my face as I moved closer to him. His guard was up; he obviously didn't trust me yet. I looked at him with calm, serene eyes to assure I meant no harm. Nothing.

I remembered Willie had asked me to feed him. Being caught up in the moment, I never did. So I changed that. I got within a meter away and then tossed him a fruit. He gulped it down in a fraction of a second. His clear, white Treye shined brilliantly. I watched him for a moment more. I closed my eyes and began to focus on his energy. I connected the two of us telepathically.

"Screech loudly. Wake them up for me!" I said to him with a comedic undertone. I opened my eyes and cracked a smile. He maintained eye contact for five more seconds and then looked up at the sky. While nearly blowing my eardrums out, he released a screech loud enough to be heard a mile away.

Regor and Willie were shocked into wakefulness, followed by my laughter. Regor's sour expression fueled my joy as it brought me back to the pranks I used to play on my brother when we were kids. He'd make that very same face.

"You scared me half to death, Wendell. You have a knack for doin' that," Willie said while sleepily glaring over at his friend. My smile lasted longer than it had in a while. It felt good. I spoke up.

"Ok. Willie. If you're not our enemy, you're going to have to prove it. Help us find our group. We have a healer. She can tend to your wounds. . . . Then we'll head towards Leumas." Willie smiled.

"Can't promise you I'll help fight Leumas. Man puts the fear of God in me. But I'll take you to 'em."

Regor darted a glance in Willie's direction, and then gave me an "are we really going to travel with this guy?" look. I nodded with a smirk.

"Do either one of you have any idea where we're going?" Regor asked with an outstretched arm. I scratched my beard in thought.

Willie spoke up to save us from confusion. "We've flown all around this area. I know where they could be." He grinned as his Treye shined. Wendell responded with a quick shriek, followed by him letting his back down.

"We're going to fly . . . on Wendell?" Regor asked.

"That's right, mate!"

Wendell let out a high-pitched squawk as I tried getting on. I could tell Regor felt a bit uneasy about it.

"I guess our suits will protect us no matter what," I mentioned matter of factly, for Regor's sake. He nodded silently.

I ran my hand over Wendell's skin. It was rough, dry, and coarse. I could feel the heat coming from his body and the energy escaping his being. He trusted us now. But mostly because Willie did.

"What about the elks?" I asked. Understanding the circumstances, they bowed their heads, and without a word, headed back toward the forest; no doubt to find the family they had left behind.

"Thank you," I said simply.

The very second we were securely mounted, Wendell let out a yell and took to the skies with a few powerful flaps of his wings. We held on as tight as humanly possible, me feeling nervous and yet oddly excited; Regor, not so much.

An hour went by on Wendell's back. Minimal small talk. A lot of thought. It was far too loud to hear a damn word anyways.

"We're here!" Willie exclaimed over the roaring wind.

We blasted downward through the clouds. The first glimpse of a pyramid felt promising.

We landed on the rough ground with a heavy thud. I was the first one to jump off, wearing my eagerness on my sleeve.

There was an eerie chill about the town. Nobody was around; there were cold gusts every so often and gloomy skies. It reminded me of a scene from an old western movie. I felt uncomfortable about it all. I called out to Leira, and then to Sandy. There didn't appear to be a single soul in the entire village. I turned back to Willie.

"Are you sure they're here?" I asked him skeptically. He replied to me without hesitation. And without a smile.

"Besides out in the savanna we just flew over . . . this . . . is the only place they *can* be." I could feel tension in his energy. He felt something was wrong, and I could do nothing but agree with him. He continued, "If they're anywhere. Anywhere safe that is . . . it has to be here. . . ."

I turned to Regor. "Do you sense anything?"

He shook his head. "They could be masking their energy. You never know if somebody who can do what I do is on their side. . . ."

I began looking into each of the eighteen pyramids. I started from the row of nine, so it took me a while to get to the first row of three. But once I got there and turned the corner, I saw something in the distance.

It was them.

I hustled over as fast as I could, calling out to Sandy and Buster. Sandy turned around with a despairing look on her face that turned into a surprised and halfway forced smile. That concerned me a bit.

I reached the group, with Regor and Willie trailing behind.

"Sam! You're alive!" Sandy said with a weakened voice. She pushed her hair back just like . . . but before I could finish my thought, I noticed that Leira wasn't among them. Neither was Kobe. This quickly turned my concern into worry.

"What could have happened?"

"Sandy . . . Buster . . . what's going on here? Where's Leira and Kobe?"

Before she could answer, Willie and Regor caught up to us. Wendell flew overhead causing their attention to shift completely. Sandy and Buster instantly jumped onto the offensive.

"What the hell is that thing?!" Buster yelled out while gripping his weapon. I was irritated by their lack of attention to my concerns.

"He's with us!" I blurted out just before repeating my initial questions. Buster turned away without a word while looking up at Wendell. Sandy looked back at me but couldn't hold eye contact. They could hear the worry and desperation in my voice; they could feel it too.

"Samuel . . ." She shook her *h*ead and said, "Dammit," to herself before continuing. "They, uh . . . they're gone."

CHAPTER 19

The Realization

I could barely put words together to make a sentence. If I had tried to speak immediately, it would have been gibberish.

After a few seconds of preparation, anger swelled up within me, forcing an aggressive response.

"Gone where, Sandy? **Where**?"

Nobody answered. I stared aimlessly at the ground in my immediate view as my anger melted into hopelessness. I let myself fall back onto the wall of the pyramid behind me. My shoulder blades pressed hard against it, but it failed to keep me standing. I gradually slid to the floor, resting my lifeless arms on top of my knees. My troubled brain painted an unsettling picture in my mind's eye. The vision burned a sizzling brand of pain into me; I was being haunted by the image already. Sandy spoke up again.

"We were in the middle of fighting off more of Leumas's soldiers. The Betas. In the middle of it, we saw him. Kobe. Running away with her. She put up a fight, but he knocked her out. . . ."

Buster began just as she finished.

"He's a coward. I would have got him myself if I would have known he was a goddamn traitor." My eyes met Sandy's again. She was nervous. Guilt-ridden even. I knew how that felt and wanted to free her of it. I knew it wasn't her fault. But I just didn't have the strength to alleviate her. I looked away.

"There wasn't anything we could do. He got us with our guards down, Samuel," Sandy added. The sound of fabric squeezing against itself let me know she had tightened her grip on her crossed arms.

Regor sensed the tension and spoke up.

"Well, let's retire here for the night. Get fully caught up, and come up with a plan for tomorrow. How's that?" Everyone nodded silently. My face was stuck in a paralyzed state of internal agony.

A warm, fiery glow projected onto that same face. The shadows it created taunted me. Fire to me always possessed an unforgiveable duality of warmth and security and yet chaotic, unpredictable destruction.

We had all shared our stories of the last two nights and gotten acquainted. I had been nearly silent the entire time. Just . . . pondering what to do. Whatever they had been saying for the last half hour had all just been muffled nonsense as far as I could tell. The muffled sounds of voices speaking turned to a ringing. A ringing that continued for a while, only progressively getting louder and louder until I tightened my fist and sat up.

"In the morning . . . I'm headed towards the mountain peak . . . to Glacial City." I was met with a moment of silence before Regor responded.

"I think you mean *we're* going to the mountain peak."

"Not this time—"

"Don't start this again. You know we—"

"NO! Regor! Everybody that follows me . . . everybody that's close to me. . . . I'm DONE. I'm just . . . I'm done." Regor walked over to me and put his hand on my shoulder.

"You listen to me and you listen intently. It's not always about **you**. Everything is not always your fault. And even if it is, that's never stopped you or the people close to you from trying to make it right." I looked back at him with tired eyes. Eyes that life had defeated many times over. Regor continued.

"Now you can try to go alone all you want. But I believe I speak for the group when I say we'll be damned if we let *you* stop us from finding Leira. And from doing what's right for *our* planet." Regor and I locked eyes. In that moment I understood.

CHAPTER 20

The Journey

We had been traveling for several days, camping out in random spots. One of us stayed up while others slept, or in my case, meditated.

We made it into two shifts. Two halves of the night was split up between two different individuals, in hopes we wouldn't get caught off guard by one of the Betas. Or any other soldiers for that matter.

Wendell flew close to the ground so as to not attract any attention from afar and was told to keep quiet from Willie. Despite the suspicions we shared about potential threats, the only true enemy we encountered were the daily drops in temperature. Since leaving the savanna, it seemed as though it had gotten at least 30-40 degrees colder. The frozen breeze consistently struck us with razor-sharp blades of wind, resulting in our suits springing into action. The material in them got far thicker, and they did an excellent job of heating our bodies. Our boots got sturdier and more equipped for the ever-changing terrain as well.

The sky glared down, dark and cloudy. It was my turn to keep watch. I sat against a thin, non-LifeTree, reflecting on the past few days of travel. After a while, I had stopped looking into the distance out of paranoia. I accepted the state we had been in, and I was doubtful we would be ambushed or spotted by anything.

I glanced over at Wendell. He helped me keep watch even though he wasn't counted on our rotation. I smiled at him and waved silently. His Treye shined brightly in the darkness as a form of acknowledgment. I had grown fond of him in the short time of our acquaintance.

My thoughts shifted to Leira. *"What can she be doing right now? What is she thinking right now? What's she feeling right now?"* These questions were open and empty. I wanted answers for them more than anything, and I felt like returning her to the group was almost as important as bringing peace to this seemingly hopeless planet. A hopeless planet that I made hopeless.

I heard a rustling in the near distance. I turned my head, knowing it was from our campsite. Buster walked his way over.

"Shouldn't you be getting some sleep? Sounds like we have a long day tomorrow," I said with genuine concern for him.

"If anyone is going to have a long day, it's you. You're the one who's going to be doing the heavy lifting."

"If by heavy lifting you meaning trying to talk some sense in Leumas, then yeah."

"Samuel . . . do you really believe that he's just going to . . . talk to you? That he's going to leave it at that? That he's just going to . . . understand you?"

"He's a piece of me, Buster. Just as you are. In that sense, all of you can understand me at some level. Wouldn't you say?"

"Understanding and agreeing aren't the same, are they?" I nodded. He was right about that.

"Wouldn't that just make me disagreeing with myself?" Buster looked at me through his rough brow. His powerful and well-shaped head looked on, as if we couldn't be more different. His fingers rubbed together in a certain familiar twitching.

"Just because we formed our consciousness from yours doesn't make us *you*." He held back a bit of resentment, but I could feel it nonetheless. His speech and understanding of consciousness surprised me. I admittedly had viewed Buster as more brutish than anything else, but it made sense when I thought deeper about it.

"*They all had access to the same information within me. They should all know everything I know,*" I thought.

"No, you're right. I guess I mean that as all humans can understand the compassion that others would have towards their young, Leumas may understand my pleas to him. They would call upon a familiar urging. A familiar sense of rationality. That's what I'm hoping for."

Buster looked at me for a moment before responding. "And yet, you're wrong again. Because we're not human."

We walked for the entire day before the winds started to pick up. Wendell was no longer able to fly; couldn't risk being seen. The closer we got to our destination, the more frequently the gusts slammed right through us. When the sun began to set, the wind quickly transitioned from periodic and mild to fierce and unstoppable. The force blowing against our direction caused us to walk slower and slower with every passing minute. The experience was rough and grueling, but we were getting through it.

Suddenly, Willie stopped us. He outstretched his hand to the right without warning. Wendell flapped his wings in a defensive action. With the constant gusts, it was hard to keep my eyes open normally. I squinted hard to look at what was in front of me, only to see crisp, white flakes delicately falling victim to the vigorous power of what was becoming a blizzard. It had begun to snow.

Willie looked back at us all. "From now on, things are about to get more intense." There was no humor in his words. There wasn't a smirk on his face, and he didn't waver in his speech pattern. He was serious. None of us moved a muscle until he did. He quickly turned back around without a reply from anyone.

The further we traveled, the more we began to feel bits of hail mixed in with the snow and powerful blasts of wind. The tough dirt we walked over slowly became slush. The slush gradually became a complete layer above the dirt. And in no time at all, we found ourselves literally stepping into the snow.

After a while, I realized there was a massive mountain range in front of us. The highest peak of the range was several times taller than the one I had encountered when I first arrived on the planet. Its immense presence reminded me of nothing other than Mount Everest.

We stopped a little under a mile away from the foot of the mountain. Willie turned around to see the group once more. He pointed out toward the area behind him. There was a steep hill preventing us from seeing what lay below. Willie spoke up.

"The Glacial City is just at the foot of the mountain in front of us. The Eye . . . is higher up. There's a separate city up top."

"Ok, now what?" Sandy asked.

"Well, a couple more steps towards the Cliffside, and they'll see us all. There's an entire army down there."

"I can feel them. There's so . . . many. . . ." Regor, Treye shining, continued after a second of thought. "Willie, our only chance is riding on Wendell's back," Regor said gently, anticipating Willie's response.

"No, no, no. We agreed I would be taking you here. This is as far as I go. Plus, you're all too heavy." There was silence. I exhaled quietly and walked over to Willie, landing a hand on his shoulder.

"Sometimes . . . we sacrifice our comfort. Our security. What we think we strive for. And sometimes that isn't the right call. Especially when done for the wrong reasons. But sometimes it's the only call. The only right one." I paused before continuing. "You broke the chains of Leumas. Escaped, seeking freedom. Now help us stop Leumas. Break the chains. Not just from yourself, but everyone else. From all the future Wendells that will roam not with a master but with a companion. With a fellow being." Willie and I shared eye contact for what felt like forever. He then darted a glance at Wendell before nodding silently.

"With this weather and our collective weight, we'll have to fly low, won't we?" Regor responded.

"So we'll be in range of arrows . . . or anything else they throw at us?" Sandy asked, slicking her hair back in a cold sweat. Willie nodded again.

"Great," Buster added. Regor took a step forward in an attempt to hold everything together.

"Unfortunately, I don't see an alternative. According to what I'm sensing, most of the soldiers are off towards the western side. So, if we fly in from the east, we'll encounter less resistance. It's our best shot." Willie then reached in his pocket and pulled out his cube.

"I have an idea regarding this little number too..." They all looked to me, as if I had the ability to take initiative.

"Well then, let us go," I said simply.

Willie walked over to Wendell and pet him affectionately over his rough-skinned hide.

"You fly well and good, mate." Wendell looked back tenderly. The depth of what they had been through together was on display in a single glance.

Wendell chirped and put his back in position.

After we all just barely fit ourselves on, we took off. We soared downward from high in the sky to swooping down to just above the city. I scanned around. The city was filled with soldiers and LifeTrees that had been picked nearly clean.

Willie pulled out his cube once more and tossed it far into the side of the city with the most soldiers present. The hologram ignited, making it appear as if Wendell was flying up above, drawing their attention. We milked that distraction as long as we could, luckily getting pretty far into the city before being noticed.

Eventually, soldiers took notice and began to fire on us with crystal arrows. They *had known* we were coming.

Wendell made sharp turns, maneuvering gracefully around the attacks and even flew between pyramids for cover.

"Look ahead! There's the base of the mountain! That trail leads you up to where the Merkaba is!" Willie shouted over the chaos.

I looked out to where he had pointed. There was an entrance guarded by Leumas's men, including Invidius, who was holding a crystal javelin. Wille, his Treye blasting a red glow, told Wendell to head straight toward them. Invidius took notice and cracked a smile before throwing his javelin with all his might.

The javelin sliced through the sky with lightning speed, finding its way directly through Willie's chest. Wendell's eyes widened in terror.

Willie flew off of the mighty creature and rolled to the snowy ground below. Wendell's shriek might as well have been a sonic boom. He made an abrupt stop to go back for Willie, causing the rest of us to fly off his back as well. I tumbled through the snow before frantically getting back to my feet.

"Willie!" I yelled. But before I could think about going back in that direction, I noticed the soldiers guarding the entrance, including Invidius, were all coming our way. Sandy and Buster got up and readied their weapons. They wanted revenge.

They deserved it.

I watched in awe as Buster and Sandy began to transform, encasing themselves in crystal as I had. Without a word, Buster took off toward Invidius. Sandy readied herself.

"Not you too. We need to plan this out!" I yelled. She shook her head in disagreement.

"No. This is something we have to do, Samuel," she replied. She spread her legs and got low.

"Now that sounds pretty familiar. Doesn't it?" She shot me a smirk. And just like that, she darted away, jumping from pyramid to pyramid, leaving afterimages behind. I glanced back over at Regor.

"We have to go after them." This time, Regor didn't contest.

Once we arrived at the battle scene, it became blatantly obvious Invidius was having trouble fending off Buster and Sandy. Buster swung his axe with ease now. Blow for blow, Invidius was getting parried and blown back by the axe's sheer power and weight.

Sandy's speed was amazing. The arrows of other soldiers missed her completely, and I could barely keep up with her movements with my naked eyes. Her crystalline suit granted her incredible agility and acrobatics as she threw small crystal darts at Invidius, slowly cracking his armor.

"We've got things covered here. Go find Leumas and Leira!" Sandy shouted.

I watched them both, wanting to but failing to come up with another solution. Other soldiers started taking notice of us and were trying to close in.

"We don't have time to think otherwise, Sam," Regor said frantically. I nodded, and we made a break for it.

A few arrows whizzed by us, and a couple of soldiers stepped in our path only to be hit by Sandy's crystal darts from afar.

Invidius saw us in his peripheral but couldn't even afford to take his eyes off of the clash for a moment.

I took one last look at Sandy and Buster, giving a mental farewell. I turned around with purpose, and Regor and I hustled up the path to the mountain's peak.

The walk up the mountain was immeasurably more difficult than any physical task I had ever done before, even with the Perceptive Suit. There was a violently wild blizzard nearly freezing our suits and blocking almost all visibility. The path up the mountain wasn't a direct one. It had constant dips, dives, and frequent climbs up with unstable footing.

I looked over at Regor. He had been right there with me the entire time without hesitation.

Suddenly, we felt a vibration from an unknown source. We stopped hiking for a moment and looked around. The two feet of snow we'd been walking in began to wet the suit reminding me to make it warmer in my ankle area. Just as I began issuing the command to my suit, I felt snow falling directly on top of my head. The blizzard was blowing damn near horizontally, so I knew it couldn't be that. Regor and I looked up slowly with open mouths. An avalanche was coming from just behind us a few hundred feet above.

We hurried up the trail as fast as we could, looking behind us every few moments. We desperately jumped from one gap in the path to the next, watching the avalanche disintegrate everything we had just climbed up.

Despite our efforts, the avalanche seemed to be catching up. We had almost reached a dead end. I could see it approaching us in the distance.

"What are we going to do?!" Regor yelled out.

"Just keep on running for now!" was all I could think of.

And that's exactly what we did. We ran all the way to the dead end, desperately looking for some way around the impasse. We only had a few more seconds before being brutally wiped out by the tremendous amount of snow and rocks falling towards us. We braced ourselves with our hands up in preparation.

Just before impact, we were scooped up by what felt like talons. I opened my eyes. It was Wendell! He shrieked with vivacious spirit. If he would have arrived even moments later, we would have been unforgivingly thrust onto the jagged rocks below. I let out a wispy breath, watching the waterfall of ice and snow fall all the way down to the base of the mountain.

Journal Entry #1001

Hey. It's uh, been a while. I abandoned this practice years ago. I think it's because I just couldn't hear myself talk about what's been happening anymore. I just couldn't bear to be alone with my thoughts. Let alone say them aloud and play them back. All I need is an echo chamber of failure. And yet here I am, magnitudes more of a failure than I ever imagined. And I'm talking about it. The tech . . . she was right to fear this all along. Maybe I should have just ignored my impulses; my ambitions. They took his designs. They used them for weapons. To try to end the war. And just like that, our world is spiraling into oblivion. I just wish I could undo everything I started. Even I'm willing to admit when I've lost control. There's just . . . nothing I can do.

CHAPTER 21

The Secret

W endell flew us all the way to the top of the mountain. There was an extremely large area of flat land and a village in the distance just before the peak.

"This is where the second Eye is. Has to be," I thought. I exhaled slowly. It was time for the confrontation.

"This is it," I said aloud, looking at Regor.

The temperature felt much warmer. The weather was still, serene, and seemingly undisturbed by the forces of nature. I peered over the edge of the mountain and saw the blizzard, still raging as far across the landscape as I could see.

I hopped off of the massive creature, looking directly into his eye. He was obviously a bit more primitive than Antler the Wise, but I could tell his feelings for Willie were strong and true. He was pincered by both the pain of loss and the love for the freedom Willie had gifted him.

I petted Wendell gently, trying to ease him by inputting the thought of "It's going to be fine. He's gone but not forgotten" into his mind. I was never really good at that stuff, but I could tell the attempt at comfort was enough for the beast. He let out a cry while looking up into the air, wings spread wide. It was the sound of sorrow itself. He knew Willie was gone, but he had to be strong and move on, for his own sake. We said our goodbyes, and just like that, he flew away.

"We're never going to see him again, are we Regor?" I said with a thin smile.

He replied after a moment of thought. "No, Sam. I don't believe so." He returned the smile.

We looked up toward the peak, trying to visualize what could be in store for us. It was night again. We had been climbing all day without rest. The moon shone brightly, beaming down enough light to illuminate everything our eyes could see and more. There wasn't a cloud in the sky either. Just the moon, Regor, me, and the path before us.

We took our first few steps toward the entrance to the city. It was truly spectacular. I noticed all of the roads, including the one leading to the first few pyramids, were tiled. The tiles were made of the crystals we had seen within the other cities before; these lit up upon stepping on them. The city was several times smaller than the first Crystal City and yet much grander. It felt ... exclusive; important even. There were actual monuments scattered around. Large crystal replicas in the shape of the Merkaba filled the centers of each crossway. The crystals growing naturally were immensely tall; some were twice as tall as the pyramids themselves. There was one in particular taller than the rest, in what looked like the center of the city.

It appeared as though there wasn't a single being around. Besides the sound of our boots hitting the crystalized tiles, the city was completely silent.

"Why would this place be abandoned?" I questioned with suspicion.

"All of those soldiers waiting for us down below had to come from somewhere, right? I bet they didn't expect us to fly over the vast majority of them with a pterodactyl," Regor replied.

I peeked my head into one of the pyramid dwellings and saw something that caught my attention. A reflection of light. I walked into the home, looking over my shoulders for any potential threats. I glanced up dead ahead of me and was taken by complete surprise. Directly behind the platform of meditation lay a mirror. As I moved closer to it, I began to realize something that startled me even further. My reflection wasn't what I had expected. I had caught faint glimpses of its light as the days had rolled on, but I guess I hadn't fully believed that I, too, now had a Treye. I watched myself move in the mirror as if I looked at someone else. I touched my forehead in near disbelief, but sure enough, the reflection showed the very same action. I turned to Regor, who was in the doorway. He stood still; watching me.

"Mirrors? I didn't see them in the other cities," I said.

He approached me while answering. "We never had them. Not before you. Not before Leumas." He could tell I was a bit disheartened by the comment and elaborated.

"Vanity hadn't even existed as a comprehendible concept. We'd simply never possessed a thought that could even lead to it. We were naked before you came here. In all ways imaginable." Again, I was silent.

"As you slept, after your time spent with the Merkaba, we collectively decided to make the Perceptive Suits. I'm aware enough now to understand why we did that. We claimed, of course, that it was to protect us from the elements. And that wasn't untrue. It did. Yet that wasn't the first thought.

"The first *instinctual* response, no, the instinct that was birthed within our psyche of conflicting dualities, was the need to cover ourselves. To protect from each other's gaze. And from the gaze of ourselves." He walked up to the mirror to take a look for himself. I paid close attention to him. His pupils dilated with curiosity as he tilted his head.

"So this . . . is how I appear. . . ." He touched his face as he said it. He shot me a glance.

"Just what have I done to this planet? To its people? I can't tell if my existence has liberated them or if it's doomed them. What does that say about me if I can't even tell the difference?" I wondered hopelessly. We were both silent, looking each other over and studying the differences between us. He spoke up again.

"Enough of this though, Sam. We came here for a reason." I nodded silently, exiting the pyramid just behind him.

We walked for a bit longer before noticing yet another peculiar and disturbing addition to the city. Bizarre statues made out of the same material as the pyramids were placed around every few blocks or so as we got deeper into the city. They were made in the image of a man with a stoic expression on his face. He was holding a small crystal Merkaba. I squinted before shooting my eyes open in terror.

It was me.

Regor looked as stunned and confounded as I was.

"What do you think this means, Regor . . . ?" I asked, nearly stuttering.

"Either they view you as a God . . . or they just have you here as a reminder of everything that opposes them."

I trembled at the thought of either one of those being true. I was brought back to what Regor had been saying in the pyramid. I shook off the thought as we pressed on.

We kept walking until we reached the city's center. A marvelous crystal grew out of the ground. It was the tallest one I had seen since I had arrived on the planet.

"Wait a second, Sam. I . . . feel something. . . . Someone is nearby. . . ." I darted my head around nervously.

Seconds later, I felt a ringing in my ears. My heart progressively pumped faster and faster. I knew what was coming next. I tried my hardest to withstand the pain of the sharp ringing, but no matter how hard I tried, I was brought to my knees once again. Regor followed a few moments after. He was squinting in pain, as I was. *"Is it Leumas again?"* I wondered.

Just then, they decided to show themselves, each coming around from a different side of the large crystal. It was two soldiers. Short, no . . . young. Not a day older than thirteen. They each grazed their fingers on the crystal as they walked, turning it a deep, crimson red, successfully bathing the entire city in its light. The ringing became less severe the closer they got to us. I studied them.

They had on identical suits; white and crystalline with one single crystal growing off of their backs. Their helmets were the same as well, sporting a perfectly spherical design with a circular visor. There was what looked like a boy, with black, shoulder-length hair thrusting out from under the visor. The other being a girl with straight blonde hair, long enough to reach her waist.

They carried guns; a planet first. They were white with a long flat barrel. They had sleek designs and were big enough to need two hands; especially for a kid. They had large crystals jammed into the bottoms where the bullet magazines would be, and the guns gave off a low hum, most likely indicating they were ready to be used at any time.

"They look a little young for a fight," I said to Regor while still looking ahead.

"It doesn't like they're going to give us a choice."

I rubbed my fingers together and tightened my fists. They slowly aimed their guns at us. We couldn't afford to make any sudden movements, but we needed to get behind cover.

We stood as still as the statues in the city, waiting for the moment to leap. And just after the very first drip of sweat fell from my temple, the crystals under the guns emanated a soft green glow. This was immediately followed by thin beams of light and an ear-shattering, high pitched, zip-like sound. They fired the first shots. Regor and I jumped out of the way just in time, crashing into the hard crystal tiling. I scurried away to get behind cover. Regor had done the same on the other side of the street.

I pushed my back up against one of the pyramids. I heard the sound of the guns being fired again. I felt one of them coming my way. I tried to transform my suit, resulting in absolutely nothing. I grit my teeth in dissatisfaction.

"This never happens when I want it to!" I screamed out over the sharp sound of the laser. The beams of light literally blew my cover to bits, and the soldier approached confidently, yet cautiously. I had to think of something.

I looked over to the street parallel to the one I had just come from. There were more pyramids, more cover, and more time to plan. I made a run for it and ducked behind cover a few pyramids away. I breathed heavily and thought quickly. I had to transform if I was to survive.

"Their guns are too powerful. They aren't using swords or bows anymore. This will kill me. And from yards away, with little to no effort or need for aim," I thought while looking down at my trembling fist.

After a few moments of near-incoherent thought, an epiphany blasted into my consciousness. The key to the suit was *necessity*. The entire time I was on the planet all I had been focusing on was what I *wanted* to do. What I wanted to change.

*"Not only is this life or death, but this is about rescuing Leira from Leumas. And stopping Leumas for that matter. I **have** to do this. I **need** to do this!"* I thought with passion laced intensity.

Crystals began to form all around my body. It was a simpler transformation; sleeker. Every one of my transformations had mimicked whatever I was up against. I fought fire with fire. In life and on this planet. *"Maybe nothing has changed in me after all,"* I thought.

My transformation was once again complete. In addition to the one crystal growing off my back like the soldier's, a rougher and more crystalized version of their gun formed there as well. I snapped it off and took a quick look at it. I had been to a few shooting ranges during my college years, but it had been a while since then.

"I'm sure this gun works the same, ..." I thought while revealing myself to the enemy. It was the boy. He had been looking behind a few pyramids and would have found me in a minute's time anyway.

We squared off with both of our rifles aimed at each other. I wanted to talk to him now. I knew he wanted to kill me and wasn't going to take lightly to the idea of conversation, but I had to give it a shot.

"I don't wanna fight you, kid," I said simply.

He didn't answer me. Instead, he fired a shot. I rolled to my right, hiding behind another pyramid.

"Not going to give me a choice," I said under my breath.

"Who are these kids? Willie didn't say anything about them," I thought. Thinking of Willie gave me an idea. It reminded me of the importance of an identity.

"Who are you?" I asked with more force behind my voice. He replied with shots to the corner of my cover once again, making the walls of the pyramid disintegrate as if they had never existed.

I was a little nervous to approach him again, but I had to keep trying. And so I pulled a fast one. I ran around to the other side of the pyramid to catch him from behind, yet as I halfway expected, he was too smart for that. He was waiting for me with his rifle aimed at my head; but unluckily for him, my rifle was also aimed at his. We both paused as we circled around each other slowly. I spoke up.

"Now I'm going to ask you once more. WHO! ARE! YOU! Tell me your NAME!" I yelled at the boy. I felt like I could have out-maneuvered him and ended it right then and there, but there was something mysterious stopping me; something I couldn't explain or understand.

He used my hesitation to his advantage, firing another few shots at me while I ran and dodged. This time one of them actually hit my leg, shattering the crystalline armor with ease. I slid behind cover again. My left leg was bleeding profusely. I couldn't move it at all anymore. I yelled out in pain as I tried to withstand how much strain it put on my mind and heart to not pass out. Whatever laser the gun used would have been powerful enough to blow my entire leg off had it not been for the crystalline suit.

I crawled over to the other side of the pyramid I was behind to buy myself a few more seconds. I told my suit to tighten around the area of the wound to stop the bleeding. Yet all the tightening and blood restriction in the world wouldn't help against the third-degree burns I now had. I grabbed my leg in excruciating pain. The soldier was seconds away from finding me, and all I could do was lay there. I had to end it. Or I would be ended.

I peeked over at the young being, resulting in a missed shot that nearly melted the entire face off of my skull.

"Think, Sam. Think," I told myself. My brainstorming was closer to a raging hurricane than it was a simple thunderstorm. I figured it out. I still had the crystal in my pocket Leira had given me. I took it out and gripped it tightly. I reminded myself they had Leira and that Kobe had taken her.

"That bastard is going to pay," I thought while tightening my grip even more, nearly crushing the crystal. *"I'm just going to have to treat this guy as if he was Kobe."*

I used the wall of the pyramid to help me stand in preparation for what I was about to do. I went to the edge of the wall and threw the crystal out in the open. He shot it out of impulse. The moment the laser collided with the crystal it was as if a thousand singular beams reflected in every direction possible. I used that distraction to slide until I was directly in front of him, and then, without a moment to spare, I fired squarely at the center of his chest. The beam sent him back a few meters into one of the statues resembling me.

I limped over to him and looked down at his body. He had a massive gash from my shot and no Perceptive suit to patch the hole. He was most likely going to die from bleeding out.

He struggled to take off his helmet unsuccessfully. I kneeled down to take a closer look at him. He coughed up some blood. He looked at me and then spoke.

"You're the . . . reason I exist," he said with strain and disdain.

"Wha-what do you mean by that?"

He used all of his strength to pry his helmet off of his small thirteen-year-old-sized head. My eyes widened in horror.

He was the spitting image of my would-be son that haunted my dreams alongside his blonde sister and Ariel.

I understood what was happening but didn't want to accept that it could be. He coughed painfully once more. I was petrified in disbelief. Tears welled up in my tired eyes.

"How . . . why . . ."

He spoke over me with a voice that had struggle and agony sewn throughout. "Tell my mother . . . I . . . I'm sorry."

"I-I . . ."

"Sorry that I couldn't make you feel the pain that she feels." The light left his eyes as his final seconds pierced me with contempt. Tears streamed down my face. I forgot about my wound. Forgot about my duty. And forgot about the moment. All I could think of was Ariel. When I left her to travel for the company. The pain I put her through. Her claiming to be pregnant. The potential family I sacrificed for my selfish ambitions.

All of it.

My entire experience on the planet had all unfolded based on the collective experience of my life and how my mind perceived it all just before going through the portal.

Roger's machine had worked exactly how it was meant to.

My now weak knees buckled, causing me to collapse. I folded over myself with lifeless limbs. Using only my trembling hands to support myself, I cried tears of anguish from grief and years of built-up regret. I bashed the ground softly with a hammer fist. I wanted it all to end. I wanted to make up for everything I had done. But I knew that was impossible.

"I'm . . . sorry. . . . I'm so very sorry," I said while sobbing. I hugged his dead corpse as I wept. It was a day I had never wanted to see come. And yet a day that had already came and went.

Regor ran up to us and asked what had happened. I explained.

"How? How did you— How did she . . ." he began to ask before stopping himself. "All we can do now is get Leira back from Leumas and put an end to this. . . . Let us go," he finished.

I looked at Regor as if it was the very first time I had laid eyes upon him. He now appeared so similar to me, and I couldn't believe I hadn't realized it all. Just as Leira represented my perception of Ariel, Regor was the embodiment of Roger.

CHAPTER 22

The End and Beginning

R egor helped me to my feet. I started to feel the burn on my leg again and grimaced in pain.

"What happened with ... the other soldier ... ?" I asked him, almost hesitant to hear the answer. He shook his head with a saddened expression. I expected that, seeing as how he still stood and she was out of sight. But I was in denial and didn't want to face the truth. I sniffled and cleared my throat. A knot of burning intensity was felt in my heart. I was angry. At myself, but also at Leumas. Angry at the fact he took my ... "children" ... and turned them against me. (Or did I?..) I didn't have much strength left, but I was determined to push through the pain and settle the score.

We made our way toward the main pyramid at the end of the city. After a bit of walking, we arrived at the entrance of the main pyramid. It was monumental. As grand as something that would be seen as a "Wonder of the World" on Earth when they still existed.

The entrance was closed, in contrast to the first Crystal City's. Yet the moment we got within a meter away, the doors of the pyramid slid independently away from each other, slowly revealing a marvelous sight.

There were hundreds of LifeTrees growing inside, shining brilliantly, with their vibrant colors radiating like neon signs. They were all encased within spherical, glass-like domes. There were thousands of crystals growing as far as the eye could see, and even some growing off of the ceiling and walls. The entire pyramid was lit up by the glow of the trees. The light refracted through the crystals, creating extraordinary patterns. The spaces in between crystals and trees were filled with countless angelic, glowing orbs created from the refraction. It was quite the sight. I noticed some of the trees were barren. They had been picked clean, dome shattered.

In the distance, we saw a single chair. There appeared to be a man sitting in the chair and a woman to his right, standing with her hands clasped in front of her waist. Behind them both was the other Merkaba. The other Eye.

"LEUMAS!" I shouted as I limped toward him.

As I got closer, I noticed the woman next to him was Leira. Her hair had grown and was now a blindingly bright blonde.

I stopped walking. Suddenly, my fist wilted into a lifeless grip.

Leumas was the spitting image of me.

From the hair, to the eyes, the stubble . . . everything I was when I first arrived on the planet. Leumas . . . was me. He rose from his throne.

"You've made it!"

Regor shifted uncomfortably. He was about to demand answers. I put a hand on his chest.

"Why? Why are you doing this?" I asked. Leumas stared at me for a few moments

"I'm only doing what you couldn't. Changing the world before me. Fixing this world," Leumas replied.

"And for WHAT?! To be revered? To be acknowledged?! . . . To be . . . *seen?*" I questioned. Leumas chuckled with closed eyes while sitting back down.

"Leira, run over here!" I called out.

She jerked as if she was about to run but was stopped by Leumas. He was controlling her with telekinesis. He pointed to the Merkaba behind him.

"Like something you can't even explain. . . . The feeling of it. But becoming one with the *second* Eye . . . changes things. Before you, we lived in the dark. But we lived in peace. And yet now that we can see, our world . . . will just dissolve in the same chaos you brought with you from your world. Your wars, your genocide. I can and I will stop it from happening. And yet you want to exercise your will on this world too. I've seen your memories. Seen your planet's history. Your history. I will prevent what destroyed your planet," Leumas explained.

"Lack of control, order. Even if I have to force it upon my people. And they are ... MY people. You? You're nothing but an outsider," Leumas continued.

"Forcing your ideology onto the world ... isn't the way. Fear ... isn't the way. If you're anything like me, you won't find peace in this ... not like this," I countered.

"You're but a human reflection of me. And nothing more. You opened our minds to that very fear. It's you who's damned us. Always was."

I watched closely at Leumas's clenched, trembling fist.

"I know I've caused this. And that I'm at fault for everything that's happened to you and to me ... but your people deserve the right to determine their own fate ... and how they wish to live. I can't ... and won't let you rule over them," I asserted.

A jet-black crystalline suit developed around Leumas.

"You won't have a choice."

Leumas then used a telekinetic wave, thrusting me into one of the glass containers around the LifeTrees, shattering it to pieces. The Perceptive Suit just barely used its sap to break the fall.

I got up quickly, hoping to dodge whatever might be coming my way, only to see Regor run at Leumas. Leumas retaliated, holding him midair telekinetically. He was crushing him. Regor began to form a crystalline suit around his feet, spreading upward. Leumas took notice and used the crystals themselves to pierce through Regor's legs. He cried out in pain.

"No!" I exclaimed.

An all-white crystalline suit grew around me, mimicking the same style as Invidius. It was too late.

Leumas slammed Regor into the ground, seemingly killing him in a single blow.

I was without breath. Without words. Without time. Leumas hurled crystals at me with his mind, some missing, some being warded off by my arm blade, and a couple making contact, forcing a few cracks in my armor.

A direct hit landed from a large shard, knocking me back into more LifeTrees. From afar, I could see Leumas casually walking over.

"Two can play at the long-distance game," I thought.

I then willed my suit to create the same bow and arrows the T. Rex rider had.

Within moments, I snapped a crystal off of my back and readied my aim. Leumas took notice, but before he could tell exactly what I was up to, I let go.

The arrow cruised toward Leumas at blinding speed, and yet it whizzed by him. He dodged at the last millisecond.

Angry now at my unpredictability, he leaped all the way over and effectively landed on top of me.

Leumas punched me square in the face with a crystal-encased fist, drawing blood.

"You don't belong here!" he shouted.

I kicked him off of me with all my might. My suit was doing everything it could, but the burn's sear was unbelievably painful. I winced.

A crystal spear formed off of my suit, like the ones the Raptor riders had. I ignored my pain and dashed at Leumas.

Leumas, using telekinesis, halted me in place. He crushed me as he did Regor. I looked up at him while in intense pain. Barely able to squeeze out a breath, I spoke.

"When we first met, you felt my pain, my regret, my inner suffering. And you took all of that on without a choice in the matter."

Leumas used telekinesis to throw me up into the air and then flung me back into the sea of LifeTrees, once again shattering dozens of casings. I lay there, motionless. I coughed a bit of blood.

Leumas held shards and crystals from all of the broken casings in midair, aimed at me. I widened my shaky, tired eyes.

"This is it. If I don't do something . . . I'm . . ."

With no time to spare, I formed the gun used by the young soldie—my son. . . . I aimed and immediately fired.

It was too fast to dodge. The laser BEAMED through Leumas's shoulder. The casings and crystals fell naturally as Leumas grunted in pain. I struggled to my feet and limped over to him.

Leumas looked me in the eyes as we locked hands, both struggling for control.

Leumas went for a punch that connected. I took it while standing still. Leumas relented for a moment. He grew an arm blade and immediately lunged it through my armor, impaling my shoulder with vigorous force.

I squinted in pain but grabbed the blade as Leumas tried to retract it. I stared down the astonished Leumas.

His **fear of me** revealed itself uncontrollably.

"Leumas! I'm . . . I'm sorry. I'm sorry that you had to end up like this . . . because of my anger and guilt that I brought with me. I'm sorry I even came here and interfered with your people," I pleaded.

Leumas's eyes widened as he stared into mine.

"It's . . . okay to want to change the world around us . . . so long as we do it for the right reasons . . . don't sacrifice what it is that we're trying to save . . . and don't lose ourselves in the process. Let me help you. Let's make a difference . . . together.'

He looked at me with eyes of understanding. My plea, understood, and from a place deep within him, acknowledged.

Leumas stepped back and looked down, drowned in conflicting thoughts. He rescinded his crystalline armor. But in that very moment, Leira **impaled** him from behind with a broken shard of my armor.

I watched him eerily fall to the ground without uttering a single sound.

"Leira . . . what are you—" I began.

She bathed in a cold, lifeless apathy. The bone-chilling gaze forced me to take a step back.

"Samuel. A single question," Leira said, her eyes leaving Leumas's dying body and finding mine. "Where are my children?"

I heard Leira's voice and Ariel's voice overlap as she spoke the last few words.

I looked back up at Leira with eyes of regret and misery. She walked closer to me.

"I made those children . . . using the second Eye. Without giving up my life. Something inside me desired to live with them. To have and be with my children. It's all I wanted. Some sort of fabricated and yet very real . . . instinct. And something inside me knew you'd take them from me."

Her Treye illuminated, forcing a vision into my head.

In the forest of dead trees, when Invidius was about to kill me, Leira and Invidius were locked in eye contact. Leira's voice echoed through my head, and yet I could tell she was telepathically speaking to Invidius.

"The truest satisfaction Leumas craves is to be tested and judged. By himself. His weaker self. That man you're killing is that very person. I will lead them all to him. And stand by Leumas's side. We want the same thing. But you must allow us to come to you. Allow us to fulfill Leumas's true wishes. All while ... beginning anew. A life of our choosing. Do you understand?"

Invidius retracted his blade from me with a "humph."

Further into the forest, Leira and Kobe collected wood for the fire. Leira's voice echoed again, this time speaking to Kobe.

"... and that's why you have to do so. I can't control myself. I'll run head first into battle. I just might throw my life away. ... Next time we encounter the enemy ... please take me somewhere else. Even if you have to carry me against my will. Will you do that Kobe? For the sake of the group? ... You're too important to risk as well. We know that." Kobe stared for a moment in contemplation. He then nodded silently.

Toward the edge of the forest, the group encountered the Betas. Leira played the victim as she was taken by Kobe. And yet when they got far enough away and out of sight, Leira swiftly cut Kobe's throat, ending his life in seconds.

She buried him under leaves and began to walk toward the mountain in the distance.

I was brought out of the visions in terror.

"But . . . why?" I asked meekly.

Leira cocked her head.

"After you refused to walk away from furthering your influence on this world, I made my decision. I needed the second Eye to make them. I knew that Leumas would try to kill you . . . and me. Stop us from coming. So I came to him. And convinced him to let you come. And I knew you would. Knew you'd lust to change this world at any cost. Take control. Just.

Like. Leumas. And when you did, I could take advantage of the opportunity," Leira revealed.

"What . . . are you talking about? What opportunity? What do you want?"

Leira's disgust was worn proudly.

"I'm going to deny you the agency. The ability to make a change on this world. Or any world. I'm going to become one with the Second Eye. And destroy it," Leira declared.

Regor crawled through the rubble, miraculously still alive.

"Regor!" I exclaimed.

"Leira. You and I both know what will happen if you do this," he said.

Leira looked down at Regor with stern apathy before turning to me once again.

"This world is beyond saving. Just like Earth was. Leumas was right about one thing. We've started on the path to becoming just like it. I will . . . end the cycle. It's people like you, Samuel, that blind the world with the light you try to shine on the shadows. Never again. Not there, or here."

"Wait!" I called out.

Leira turned around and began the process of becoming one with the Merkaba.

"Goodbye," her voiced echoed the last word I said to Ariel as I walked away from her all those years ago.

I started after Leira.

"What are you doing, Samuel!?" Regor asked.

"I . . . have to stop her. I have to try."

"But if you go after her, you'll be trapped in there with her. Even worse, it'll—"

"I JUST WANT TO MAKE THINGS RIGHT FOR ONCE! I just . . . want to make it all end. Not for me, for my sake. But for everyone else. And if nothings left of me. . .then at least I paid for it. For it all. And died *trying*." Regor looked into my soul, deeply understanding me like never before.

"Alright, Sam."

I ran over to the large crystal. It was already spinning fast enough for the Eye to appear. I looked back at Regor with a genuine smile.

"See ya, Roger, once again."

A small tear slid down Regor's left cheek. It reflected the light emitted from the Merkaba.

I turned away, reached over, and ascended to the Eye. In that moment, as I was being absorbed into the vast vessel of energy that was the second Eye, I realized the hand within the crystal armor, the vision I had seen within the first Merkaba, was just me. It was my hand, in this moment.

Within seconds, I was atomized. One with it all, as Leira was. Leira, my consciousness's perception on how Ariel felt all these years. The embodiment of my perspective of the pain I caused her.

The Merkaba spun faster and faster. The LifeTrees shone so bright that it was all that could be seen. The Merkaba broke apart slowly and then exploded in an energetic EMP.

The glacier behind the mountain splintered and then fully cracked in a devastating chain reaction. And like a levy breaking, a world-ending flood poured in and drowned the planet in its entirety. Instead of merely ending the cycle, my influence ended it all.

"There was nothing I could do. Nothing I could have ever done. Nothing to outrun what's already done."

Roger's machine worked as intended.

The passage of time flowed at impossible speeds from the moment after the explosion, to an ice age, to flourishing plant life, to evolution of primitive animal life, to dinosaurs, to eventual human evolution.

A young Roger Kaine finds a crystal in the ground at an expedition. It resonates with his soul and forces his eyes wide open. Not merely a crystal. **A shard from the Merkaba.** It's the crystal that powers the machine that I will use ~~have used~~.

It was Earth. Always Earth. Always within me. Never separate. Never could be.

ABOUT THE AUTHOR

I grew up in and around Miami, Florida. I was raised by two powerfully inspiring parents who always supported the idea of creative writing. From a father who wrote and produced 200+ songs, to a mother who read and told stories to me throughout childhood, I've always been surrounded by creative energy.

It's my passion to bring stories to life while containing valuable meaning between the lines of subtext. Every project gets us one step closer to making this world a better place through thoughtful art and meaningful conversation that's born of it. My goal is to have the audience walk away with more than they came with; and I aim to give people something to think about or, at the very least, be wildly entertained.

01010100 01101111 00100000 01100010 01100101 01100111
01101001 01101110 00100000 01110100 01101000 01100101
00100000 01101000 01110101 01101110 01110100 00100000
01100110 01101111 01110010 00100000 01100001 01101110
01110011 01110111 01100101 01110010 01110011 00101100
00100000 01100101 01101101 01100001 01101001 01101100
00100000 01101001 01101110 01110100 01110010 01100001
01100001 01110011 01110000 01101001 01100011 01101001
01100001 01110100 01000000 01100111 01101101 01100001
01101001 01101100 00101110 01100011 01101111 01101101
00100000 00100010 01001001 00100000 01110111 01101001
01110011 01101000 00100000 01110100 01101111 00100000
01110011 01100101 01100101 00100010

www.ingramcontent.com/pod-product-compliance
Lightning Source LLC
Chambersburg PA
CBHW020602180626
46810CB00007B/2613